WHAT HAPPENS WHEN YOU'RE
YOUNG,
SCARED,
BROKE
AND ON YOUR OWN?
. . . WHEN YOU'RE

MR. and MRS. BO JO JONES?

MR. AND MRS. BO JO JONES
is an achingly familiar story in count-
less American homes. The bride is six-
teen and pregnant, the groom is seven-
teen and astonished.

They're thrown together in a marriage
of necessity which abruptly abbreviates
the education—and social life—of both;
which thrusts the football hero and his
child-wife into a play house with real
problems, into a new adulthood where
kids have to grow up fast.

mr. and mrs.
BO JO JONES

ANN HEAD

A SIGNET BOOK
PUBLISHED BY THE NEW AMERICAN LIBRARY

Library of Congress Catalog Card Number: 67-15109

This is an authorized reprint of a hardcover edition
published by G. P. Putnam's Sons.

SEVENTH PRINTING

SIGNET TRADEMARK REG. U.S. PAT. OFF. AND FOREIGN COUNTRIES
REGISTERED TRADEMARK—MARCA REGISTRADA
HECHO EN CHICAGO, U.S.A.

*SIGNET BOOKS are published by
The New American Library, Inc.,
1301 Avenue of the Americas, New York, New York 10019*

FIRST PRINTING, MAY, 1968

PRINTED IN THE UNITED STATES OF AMERICA

To My Daughters Nancy and Stacey

With much talk about teen-age marriages, I feel, for whatever it may be worth to some young couple on the brink of same, that I should tell about mine.

I was sixteen, and Bo Jo was seventeen when we got married. As the statistics say, most teen-agers who marry, marry because they have to. Or else. We looked into some of the "or elses" and decided they weren't for us. Maybe marriage wasn't either. But at least it was a positive thing to do. And everything else looked negative.

There was nothing offbeat or way-out about either of us or the crowd we went with at Trilby High. There was a fast crowd. There is in every high school. But we got our kicks from Joan Baez records, J. D. Salinger, pizza, and foreign films, and our word for the ones that went for booze, making-out, and souped-up cars was "infant."

Bo Jo was all lined up for State U in another year, with the help of a football scholarship, and my parents had me slated for my mother's alma mater, a girls' college in New England, if I could make the grade. The way my marks shaped up it looked as though I would. I'm no great brain, but I've got a busy memory, and I just plain *like* certain subjects like English Lit and biology, when it isn't dissecting frogs. All that helps. So we both had good solid plans for the future, and we weren't going steady. The subject never came up and if it had we probably would have both said we didn't believe in going steady, though we were seeing more and more of each other and less and less of everybody else as time went on. I admit I was fairly well snowed, but I'd been snowed before and managed to hang on to my common sense, not to mention my ideals. But Bo Jo was different from anybody I'd ever dated. He seemed older for one thing and more sure of himself. He had reason to feel sure of himself. He was not only Trilby High's star halfback, but he did very well in track too, and his marks, with the exception of English, were pretty good even though he worked after school and weekends at the supermarket when he wasn't in training. The boys I'd been used to dating were boys I'd grown up with. Their parents knew my parents, and although Tommy Ryan and I had parked once or twice on the way home from the movies and I don't know anybody I'd rather dance with then Julius Spence, I still think of them more as brothers than anything else. Not so Bo Jo.

For one thing Bo Jo kept his thoughts to himself so I never really knew how he felt about me, if I was making the grade with him or if he was still remembering Alicia Helms, whom he used to go with before her family left town. The big thing, of course, was how I felt when Bo Jo was around. All there and all gone. That way of feeling coupled with a lot of little things like the champagne somebody smuggled into the punch at the junior-senior prom that night and Alicia Helms back in town again trying to rebuild a fire between herself and Bo Jo is what caused my downfall, if you want to call it that. And I do because up until that night I'd always had strong ideas and opinions about love and marriage and waiting until the two coincide, and what happened with Bo Jo didn't change them.

After a party, if it wasn't past curfew time, which for most of us was twelve on weekends, a gang of us usually went to the Coffee Pot or someone's house and played records and ate hot dogs or hamburgers, but that night Bo Jo and I rode out to the beach instead. I'd never been to the beach that late at night unless there was another couple along. It was a kind of unspoken rule among us, but it was a beautiful night and I was feeling lighthearted and festive, and besides, anywhere else we went, Alicia would probably be there so when Bo Jo said, "Let's go have a look at the ocean," I don't even remember feeling daring about it or giving it a thought one way or another. I trusted Bo Jo. I trusted myself. I had no idea that there actually *is* a point of no return.

Afterwards I was shattered. And furious with Bo Jo. And furious with myself. In fact, only my pride held me together and kept me from bawling like a baby all the way home that night. Now that I know Bo Jo better, I think he was upset too, but he didn't act it, and when he left me at my house, I didn't care if I never saw him again. That was a Friday night. He didn't call Saturday, and by Saturday night I was a wreck thinking about what he must think of me and how I might not ever see him again. It was a new and terrible way to feel, because I was the one who had played it cool and hard to get. I felt deeply humiliated. I wasn't furious with Bo Jo anymore. Or wouldn't be if he'd just call.

Sunday he called as though nothing had happened, and we went to the movies Sunday afternoon as though nothing had happened. But he didn't put his arm around me when the lights went down the way he used to, and we didn't laugh at the corny love scenes the way we used to. I wondered if that was good or bad.

Afterwards we went to a drugstore and sat in one of the back booths, and after Bo Jo had looked around like a hood casing the joint, he said, "I'm sorry about the other night, July. I can't even tell you ... I hope you aren't mad."

I didn't know what I expected him to say, but I felt let down.

I said, "Do I act mad?"

"You don't act happy."

"I'm not," I said. "I never thought in a million years that I ... I mean I've always felt superior to the kind of girls ... well, no, I'm not happy. Not in the least, as a matter of fact."

"It was that damned champagne somebody slipped in the punch. It'll never happen again. I promise." He sounded beat.

"I don't think we ought to go on dating," I said, because I knew it wasn't just the champagne. It was the way Bo Jo had made me feel.

"But there's no other girl I want to date," he said. And I couldn't help thinking, well, at least that closed the book on Alicia Helms. It was the first halfway cheerful thought

9

I'd had in days. "Is there anybody else *you* want to date?" He looked worried.

I took time out to let him worry, but the truth was that I'd lost interest in other boys.

"Offhand I can't think of anyone," I said.

"Then let's not be chicken. Just because we fell off the deep end once ... it doesn't mean it will happen again. I'm crazy about you, kid, I really am, and I won't let it, I promise."

We shook hands on it. We honestly believed it never would happen again. And it didn't. Not for a long time. But our mistake was in thinking you can make a relationship between two people go backward. Or stand still. Or take orders from headquarters. Meaning the brain.

Well, that's the background.

The preface, you might say.

At first I pretended I'd got my dates mixed up. It's surprising the power of wishful thinking when that's all that's standing between you and absolute chaos. But the pretending didn't hold for long. One day right in the middle of English class I got scared. For no reason at all. I'd only been scared twice before in my entire life. I mean the cold terror variety when your heart starts up and your mind stops. But both those times there had been a reason. Once I saw my mother thrown from a horse, and another time a man tried to break into our house when our parents were away and the sitter had gone out to mail a letter. If it hadn't been for those two experiences I wouldn't have known what I was feeling there in English class. I would have thought I was dying. As it was, I thought maybe I was going crazy. There was nothing and no one in that entire room to scare anybody, and there I sat shaking like a leaf. It didn't last long. Probably only a few seconds. But it happened again that very night at the supper table while I wolfed down my favorite dessert ... apple brown Betty with hard sauce ... and again the next morning in the shower, but by that time I faced up to what was spooking me. Not that that helped much, but at least I wasn't going off my rocker. I had a reason to be scared. One of the best. I cried awhile in the shower with the noise of the water to drown out the sound of me and wished there was somebody I could talk to. Somebody who wouldn't be shocked or hurt and would know what to do next. Somebody entirely unlike my mother or my father or Mary Ann Simmons, my best friend.

Realizing that I couldn't talk to Mary Ann really struck me where I live. Even though we were entirely different kinds of people, I'd never done anything in my life or had anything happen to me before that I couldn't tell her about if I felt like it. But this I knew would just knock her for a loop. For a girl who has been brought up in an atmosphere of pseudo-sophistication she is terribly naïve and, corny as it may sound, pure. I suppose that's the sort of wall she had to build around herself to keep her balance in the midst of all her father's divorces and remarriages and the dozens of children he acquired along the way. He seems to have a weakness for fertile women with no maternal instincts, and he always gets custody of the children when they leave him. Not only his own but theirs by whatever former marriages they've had. Mary Ann calls them "the orphans" and gets them out of the house when her father and current stepmother have parties and generally tries to protect them from the facts of life. Her own mother was a Clyburn from Virginia, of which Mary Ann is very proud, though that is just about all she knows about her because she remarried almost immediately after the divorce and went to live in Peru. I don't think Mary Ann hears from her very often, if at all.

We've been friends, Mary Ann and I, ever since first grade. Our fathers went to boarding school together and then to college and though Father thinks Mr. Simmons could have managed his life a lot better than he has, he is very fond of him in a paternal sort of way, and they belong to all the same clubs. I vaguely remember Mary Ann being brought to our house on Sunday afternoons now and again and left there to share our nurse while our parents went off somewhere together. I even think I remember on one of those occasions taking scissors and cutting off some of her curls because I couldn't stand the fuss everybody made over them. Mary Ann says it was someone else. She can't bear to carry a grudge for two minutes or be mad for five. I, on the other hand, enjoy a black rage now and then. I suppose that's why we get

11

along so well together. We complement each other, and we don't compete with each other for the simple reason there's nothing to compete about. We're both A-one students, our families both live in South Edge, which isn't a place at all but just a name given the part of town where most of the old and established families live. We are both majorettes in the high school band. She is blond and pretty and gentle. I'm red-haired, green-eyed, and "spirited" is how the Trilby annual put it. And the sort of boys that appeal to me don't appeal to her and vice versa, which makes for a good relationship, especially in high school. She likes the skinny sensitive types who send flowers and play games with "the orphans" and write for the school magazine and ask her to wait for them until they finish college. Naturally I'd like to get flowers now and then too, but the type of boy I like just doesn't think flowers. He thinks sports and doing things with his hands, making things, taking them apart. I always thought there was something lacking in a boy who couldn't take a car apart and put it together again, though I don't know why. My father doesn't know a filter pump from a carburetor, and I think he's the greatest. I also like a boy to have a good physique, and Mary Ann never cared how a boy looked as long as he had "quality." She used the word very loosely. It could mean anything from a way with girls to a real honest talent of some kind. When I first started dating Bo Jo, she wanted to know what I saw in him. I said for heaven's sake wasn't it obvious. I saw what half the girls in Triby High saw and wanted—a real go go guy with a lot of future.

"I know all that," Mary Ann said. "He's attractive-looking and a big wheel on the football team, but so are half a dozen other boys. What's Bo Jo's quality?"

To her I said, "For heaven's sake, who cares? He's nice and he's fun and *he* likes *me*." But I did think about it afterwards. It was a good question. Especially as I'd never had so much going for a boy before. I decided one day watching him at football practice that his "quality" was persistence. He wasn't as heavy as a lot of the other boys on the team nor was he, with his broad chest and short stocky legs, built for speed, but when he tackled a guy the guy knew he'd been hit, and when he ran he was not easy

12

to catch up to. Wherever he'd got with the team, he'd had to do some long-range planning and put in a lot of tough body work. It was the same with his grades. There wasn't a subject except geometry that came easily to him, but he was hell-bent on a college education, and the way his parents were fixed, or weren't fixed, he'd never make it without a scholarship, and he couldn't even make a football scholarship without grades. This persistence carried over into everything he did, whether it was courting a girl or changing a tire, and you felt it as a kind of power, a kind of strength in him that most other kids his age didn't have. Manly is the word I used when I thought about him in those days before I knew I would ever have to put him to the test.

However, it wasn't Mary Ann's not seeing Bo Jo in his best and true light that made it impossible for me to tell her what had happened now. I couldn't tell her because she was in love. I mean really. In an adult way. He was older, a junior in college, and already she was pinned to him. She would never in this world understand this type of problem. Not now. Not anymore. And knowing her, she would probably cry if I told her about it.

Realizing that I couldn't talk to the people who really mattered to me made me cry harder. Of course there was Bo Jo, but we'd had a fight the week before, and I didn't want to say anything to him until I absolutely had to. Until I was sure. The truth was we hadn't been getting along lately. I was still crazy about him, and I'm pretty sure vice versa, but my opinion about love and marriage hadn't changed, only my opinion about myself, and I knew we ought to break up. Bo Jo knew it too. That wasn't *what* we fought about, but it was *why* we fought. The wanting to break up and the not wanting to.

I put drops in my eyes and painted over the red rims with eyebrow pencil and got through breakfast without notice.

Bo Jo and I didn't have any classes together, but we did have a study hall at the same time and always sat at the same table. Talking was out, but sometimes we managed to sneak a note or two without old Eagle Eyes McPherson, the librarian, swooping down. That day Bo Jo was late getting there. Usually I gave him the "hi" sign with

13

my eyes, but that day I felt strange with him and nervous and kept focused on a page of Latin verbs. I could feel he was excited about something the way he sat down without first putting down his books and began writing something fast on the back of an envelope. He shoved the envelope at me without bothering to see if Eagle Eyes was watching. What he'd written was *This calls for a celebration.* The envelope came from the Director of Admissions at State U, and inside it was a letter saying that his application for an athletic scholarship had been passed on by the Board contingent on (their words, not mine) his attending summer school for the summer preceding his entry in order to bring up his English grades which to date did not meet with the college requirements. I wrote back *Wonderful* under what he'd written, made like a smile, and went back to the Latin verbs, which were jumping around on the page like Mexican jumping beans. I thought that when the bell rang I was going to have to come up dispensing enthusiasm or some reasonable facsimile thereof, but I was wrong. Bo Jo was so far out on cloud nine that I could have been crying my eyes out and he wouldn't have noticed. His father never got to go to college, and the Joneses aren't exactly loaded with cash even now, so the whole college bit meant everything and then some to Bo Jo. He was going to physics class and I to English so we separated at the water cooler. "I'll see you tonight," he said. "I've already got Charlie working on the celebration ... Savannah no less ... the Reef ... Pick you up about eight." He grinned and loped off down the hall without a care in the world.

It depressed me to think that only a few weeks ago I would have been mad for a night at the Reef with Bo Jo. It would have represented the absolute ultimate. I'd never been to Savannah with Bo Jo, not even to a movie, and I'd only been to the Reef once in my whole life ... with a gang of kids, dutch ... it was THE place of that year and well worth the two-dollar cover charge. If you had it. I guessed tonight Bo Jo must be busting into his college bank and I really shouldn't let him, if what I thought was so, was. Not only that, I didn't see how I was possibly going to get decked out in the mood Bo Jo would expect me to be in. I even thought of calling him that afternoon

14

and telling him I couldn't go, that I was sick, which at that point wouldn't have been too far from the truth, but then I remembered what a big moment this was for him and how he might not have another one for a long, long time if at all, so I decided to go through with it. All the way.

We took two cars because there were eight of us. The usual crowd minus Mary Ann and plus Alicia Helms, who was with, of all people, Rodney Blue, which meant that she'd been determined to horn in on the celebration whatever the price. Not that we don't all adore Rodney, but he's sort of the court jester type, the extra man that we all lean on and tell our troubles to and include in on everything we do but we just don't date Rodney except out of sheer desperation. In the first place, he never asks any of us for a date, so if we are desperate it means asking him and while he's always more than willing, it's not the same as being asked by someone special. Though Rodney is lots of fun, in a crazy kind of way, and adds a lot whenever he's along, going out with him takes the edge off of everything. He simply isn't that interested in you. His mind is always on something else, music, photography, or how to commit the perfect crime, and he's not very attractive physically. He has "handsome" eyes as my mother says, but he's skinny and pale and walks as though his joints are tied together with elastic. He has never as far as I know made a pass at any of us, though he does show up now and again with some real sexy-looking little freshman or junior high-er, and I imagine he probably makes passes at them. I was afraid he and Alicia would be riding with us in Charlie Saunders' car. I was afraid Alicia would have worked it that way. She knows Charlie and Bo Jo are best friends, so that would be whose car we'd be riding in. She tried but Rodney put his foot down. Six in one car was too many, he said, and just because Tommy Ryan and Boots wanted to be alone was no reason why they should be.

Charlie Saunders is the only one in our crowd that is the least bit wild, but he's quiet about it. Whenever he wants to "throw one" he does it out of town at one of these little joints that nobody we know ever goes to and, unlike the beatnik types we know, keeps it to himself

15

afterwards. I would never guess if Bo Jo hadn't told me. However, my parents must have an instinct for that kind of thing because the two or three times Charlie has come to the house with Bo Jo to pick me up, they've been just short of rude to him. Not that Charlie would notice. He thinks everybody thinks he's great and that the whole world is his oyster. Weekends he ushers at the Arcadia, all dressed up in tight blue pants and red coat with gold braid across the front of it and looks like the Student Prince himself. I didn't like him, but I pretended to because of Bo Jo, because of their closeness. As a matter of fact, I think if I hadn't pretended to, back there in the beginning when Bo Jo and I first started going together, I doubt if Bo Jo would have kept on going with me. I don't know what it is he and Charlie have going, but when they're together they act like two kids on a picnic. My mother says she has never known what makes for friendship between men and has often wondered, since it doesn't seem to have anything to do with what they have or don't have in common or anything at all that you can pinpoint. A lot of them don't make any sense to anyone else and last for a lifetime. Whatever I felt about Charlie I didn't ever dare say anything to Bo Jo about him that wasn't highly complimentary.

Charlie's date that night was Gail Hyatt, for which I was grateful because she talks a lot so at least on the ride over no one would notice if I didn't.

The Reef is located in what used to be an old warehouse down on the canal front. The street that runs along the canal has never been paved. It is still a mixture of bricks and cobblestones and death on tires. We parked a couple of blocks away because Charlie didn't want to take any chances with his father's new Bonneville. Crossing the streets Bo Jo took my arm. In Trilby the traffic is no hazard, and Bo Jo had had no occasion to be protective in this way before. After the weeks of worrying and misery the feel of his hand on my arm guiding me across the wide street was reassuring. His hands are square and firm and when I thought about them they always gave me a feeling of confidence in him.

Tommy Ryan, who drives like he was testing out for the 700, and the others were waiting for us outside the

16

entrance. We hoped to all sit at the same table, but none of us had been there enough times to be sure about anything. Inside it was huge and dark, darker than it had been on the street where there had been streetlights. Inside the Reef the only light came from the candles that stood one each table and the slice of light that splashed through the door when the waiters came through from the kitchen.

"I need my scuba glasses," Rodney muttered. I knew what he meant. It was a little like being underwater. The darkness and the layers of drifting smoke and the huge shadows that moved against the wall.

We couldn't get a table all together, but we got two tables for four right next to each other. This time Alicia made it. I don't know quite how she did it, but when we sat down she and Rodney were at our table and Charlie and Gail at the other one with Boots and Tommy. Before I'd started going with Bo Jo, I could take Alicia or leave her alone, but since I started going with him everything about her irritated me. Her face for one thing, baby blue eyes and lips that looked as though they'd just been kissed or were waiting to be, and her clothes for another. For instance, that night the rest of us were wearing flats and skirts because that was the sort of place the Reef was, and Alicia knew it, but she had on shoes with tiny heels and a dress that wasn't so too much that it was out of place, but it made us look like a bunch of schoolgirls.

There was a three-piece combo that sat around a table in the middle of the place and played and every hour or so Shuford Foard would come on with his guitar and sing for a while. He was the main reason we came. He sang the kind of songs that all the other folk singers at that time were singing through their noses, only he sang them from the back of his chest cavity, making up his own lyrics as he went along. He really could move you where you lived. There wasn't any dancing because there wasn't any room for it. The place was filled up with tables and the tables stayed filled up, and from about eleven on there were people waiting outside and the waiters began giving you dirty looks if you weren't eating or drinking something more in spite of the cover charge and what you'd eaten and drunk before.

"The thing to do," Alicia said, when the boys began to

anxiously study the menu, "is stall over your order. Tell 'em you'll wait a little while, that you just had supper."

"Jeeze," Rodney said, "you sound like you have lived here." Which, of course, was just what she'd wanted him to say, or someone to say.

"It was ages ago," she said, looking not at Rodney but at Bo Jo, "when I went with that Duke boy . . . you remember him, Bo Jo, you almost knocked his teeth out once."

"That's right, so right," Bo Jo reminisced happily. "But I can't remember why . . . what it was all about." He scowled, trying to remember above the noise of the combo and the people talking around us.

"It was about me," Alicia said. "He wanted me to go home with him. . . ."

"Oh, that's right," Bo Jo said matter-of-factly. "Only I'd brought you. One of life's little triumphs." He looked at me and grinned and put his hand over mine on the table. "Wish you could have been there to see it. First and last time, probably, that I ever landed a right to the jaw. I was just mad enough to do it. Just mad enough. . . ." Obviously Bo Jo hadn't the remotest idea where Alicia had been trying to lead him. That's one of the nice things about boys. They just don't dig the furtive nuance. But I did, and I gave her a look that told her so. But there was no pleasure in winning the round. The cat game was new to me, and win or lose, I didn't like it. I always used to take the attitude that any girl who'd show her claws over a man better start looking for another one.

"Why so pensive, kid?" Bo Jo said.

Between the asking and the answering I lived and died a thousand truths—"Because I'm feeling insecure, to put it mildly". . . . "Because I can't go back and I don't want to go forward". . . . "Because all of a sudden this music is making my head ache and the sight of Alicia is making me sick to my stomach". . . . "Excuse me," I said to Bo Jo. "I've got to go to the girls' room. I drank that Coke too fast. . . ."

I barely made it and then only to the washstand . . . all the little doors begged for dimes, and by the time I'd found a dime it would have been too late. There was someone else at the other basin, but I couldn't help that.

When I could say anything at all, I said, "I'm sorry, please excuse."

"Since when did they start serving drinks to minors in here? I thought the place was strictly legal." Her voice was husky, languid. I looked at her. She was skinny, and her hair was piled high on her head, black hair, with a couple of combs holding it in place. Her eyes too were black, and she'd painted more black around them, but even with all the blackness and the low-cut dress she wore and the wedding ring on the hand that she raised to pat her hair into place, she didn't look much older than I. Eighteen at the most, I figured, and wondered what she was doing all dressed up like somebody's call girl and married to boot.

"They are legal," I said. Maybe she was a spy for some law enforcement unit. "What made me sick was Coke . . . I drank it too fast."

She looked me over then and deciding, apparently, to believe me said, "I hope it wasn't the hamburgers. I just ate three."

"We haven't ordered yet," I said. "It had to be the Coke."

"Well, that's a relief." She smiled a surprisingly little-kid smile, crooked teeth and all, and went on out. I combed my hair and washed my face and put on fresh lipstick and when I got back to our table I saw that the girl I'd met in the powder room was at the microphone beside Buddy Lars, who leads the combo, and he was getting ready to introduce her. Charlie and Bo Jo and Alicia were talking so I said "Shush" because I wanted to hear who she was.

"Every night, as you know," Buddy Lars was saying, "someone from the audience gets a chance to show us what they can do. Tonight our choice, and it wasn't easy, so many of you with all kinds of talent . . . tonight our choice was"—he waved a hand to silence those who were still talking—"this little lady here beside me, Lou Consuela, Mrs. Nicolas Consuela, to be exact . . . and that's her husband over there at that table against the wall, all two hundred and ten pounds of him in case any of you young bucks get any ideas."

I looked where his hand directed, but it was too dark

19

and smoky to see anything but the outline of a man's head and shoulders in the distance.

". . . Lou Consuela and she's going to sing a little song she composed herself." Shaking her head the girl leaned toward him and whispered something. "Begging your pardon, she didn't compose the music," Buddy amended, "just the lyrics. The music is by Brahms, no less, Johannes Brahms himself."

Rodney, at the next table, muttered, "This I gotta see." Brahms is his favorite classical composer. Charlie Saunders whistled under his breath as the spotlight moved to Lou's face, and Bo Jo said to whoever was listening, "Why waste all that sex on Brahms!"

"I think I've seen her some place before," Alicia said.

"*Shhhh,*" I said again. "I want to hear. . . ."

What she sang was the Brahms lullaby with a hip beat and her own words. "So good night, but do not sleep . . ." not downright sexy but suggestive. Her voice did the rest. Her voice was low and beguiling and someone had taught her how to use it. Rodney said you could tell by the way she breathed . . . her timing of a note. Rodney clapped until I thought he'd get blisters on his palms. He wanted to hear her sing something else. She came back to the mike, but she sang the same song all over again, which was a letdown. By that time the waiter had brought our hamburgers, and we couldn't put off eating them any longer. We could see that there were people waiting for tables, and none of us had the nerve to dawdle over our food.

We drove home with Tommy Ryan and Boots Levy. I managed that by simply climbing into the back seat of Tommy's car when we got to the parking lot. Charlie looked hurt and annoyed. He can't stand Rodney. He says he reminds him of a schoolteacher he had in the first grade.

I drove home in the crook of Bo Jo's arm and listened to him and Tommy discussing spring track as though it were the most important thing in the world. They were, in fact, so hot on the subject of whether or not Tommy would make all-state that Bo Jo could hardly bring himself to break away long enough to take me to my door, much less go through the door and into the hall where he could kiss me good night.

"It was a simply marvelous evening," I said. "A wonderful celebration!"

"Sure thing," he said.

"Well, good night."

"See you tomorrow."

I should have let him go back to the car and Tommy and the track right then, but he looked so free, so impatient to be off about his business, I couldn't stand it.

"When tomorrow?" I said. "Where?"

He looked at me as though he thought I'd lost my mind. "Second period. In the library," he said, "like always."

But of course that wasn't what I'd meant. I was sick once more in my own bathroom before I went to bed. "The time has come the walrus said . . ." The quotation ran through my head like a tune that refuses to be replaced. "The time has come . . ." It made a kind of rhythm in my head that after a while was actually almost soothing. "The time has come the walrus said." It must have stayed with me in my sleep, gently compelling me, for the next day after school I hopped a bus for Westcott, which is about fifty miles away, bought myself a wedding ring at the dime store, and picked a doctor out of the telephone directory. He turned out to be a heart specialist, which wasn't too unrelated to my problem, but he did know a few facts of life besides. He wasn't fooled by the wedding ring or by the phony name I gave with the "Mrs." attached. He said he had a daughter just about my age. He told me to go home and tell my parents the truth and not to waste any time. He said that was what he would want his daughter to do. But I wasn't his daughter, and he didn't know my parents. My mother is a quiet, well-bred type, descended from a long line of quiet, well-bred types, judging from my Boston grandmother and Great-Aunt Susan, of Cambridge, Mass. She is tall and slender with long hands, long feet, brown hair parted in the middle, and clear, brown, unafraid eyes. She likes horses and big dress-up parties and biographies of famous men and lilac perfume and tea with breakfast. My father is a lot older than she and very handsome and reserved.

He married late. My Grandmother Greher says he was much too comfortable living at her house and being eligible and sought after. Mother, she says, bowled him over the minute they met. He still treats Mother as though she'd come in a velvet-lined box with a Tiffany label, and always speaks of us as "Agnes' children," as though that made us terribly special. I'm not in the least like either of them. I am small and red-haired and cat-eyed and moody, and when I was little I used to get furious at people who said, "Where on earth do you suppose she came from, Agnes?" I don't anymore. I like having my own identity and not being lumped into the mold like my younger sister Grace, who is a born lady like Mother, and Gregory, who looks like Father and when we go to church copies the way he walks.

When I was little, my hope and ambition was to grow up to be just like my mother, but looking back on it, I think that was more because of the way I felt about my father than because of how I felt toward her. He so obviously thought she was the greatest, and I thought he was the greatest and therefore ... Not that I don't still admire my mother very much, but I've learned there are other men in the world besides my father and that trying to be like someone you aren't in the least like is what makes people go schizoid.

Mother and I get along as well as most and better than some. Or did until I started dating Bo Jo. The worst of it is I could understand why she had this thing about him. She has led a very sheltered life, Father too actually, if by sheltered you mean the opposite of exposed. The first date Bo Jo had with me he just drove up to the house to get me and never got out of the car. Honked the horn. I can see Mother's face now. More astonished than anything else.

"Surely that's not someone blowing for you," she said.

"It's Bo Jo Jones," I said. "I told you I had a date with him tonight." I was blushing like a fool. . . .

"Bo Jo? What an odd name." She looked perplexed as well as astonished. "Do I know him?"

"It's short for Boswell Johnson, and no, I don't think you do. They haven't lived here long." I inched toward the door while she went to the window and looked out.

"I can't see anything from this distance," she complained. "Do you suppose if you didn't come right away he'd just sit there . . . or, or drive away?"

"He'd probably blow again," I said. "Anyhow, goodbye, see you at eleven. . . ." It was what I always said.

"Wait a minute," Mother said. "I've a message for your friend out there. Tell him that we like to meet the boys you go out with *before* you go out with them."

"Oh, Mother, please, not tonight. You can meet him next time"

"Are you ashamed of him?"

"Lordy no! He's *the* big man at school this year, football, track, student council. I've been dying for a date with him for ages. Please don't spoil it."

"If meeting your family is going to spoil . . . oh, well . . ." She shrugged. "But see to it that he minds his manners in the future."

"He's a great friend of Tommy Ryan's," I said, "and Rodney's." I hoped that would appease her somewhat.

When I asked Bo Jo why he hadn't come to the door to pick me up, he said that he'd quite honestly had no idea the kind of neighborhood I lived in or that the house would be so big. He said it hit him out of the blue. Scared him. He said he just did what seemed like the easiest thing at the time, which was to blow. I said I hadn't minded, but my mother had.

"I'll tell you one thing," Bo Jo said. "Your mother is going to mind just about everything about me. I think you ought to know that right from the start."

And he was so right. Bo Jo wasn't her type. The only boys she knew when she was growing up in Boston went to prep school and came home just long enough over the holidays to take her to dances and get stewed, and all that mattered was whether or not they were smooth, whatever that meant in Boston all those long years ago.

Actually I suppose I get along better with Father for the simple reason that he thinks I can do no wrong. I am, in short, the apple of his eye. He and Grace have more in common because they both collect stamps and he and Gregory do more things together because Gregory is a boy, but I know by the way I feel when he looks at me or talks to me that I am it as far as he is concerned. Not that he loves me more than the others. It's more a pride kind

23

of thing. And it wasn't going to do me any good now. Or him.

Riding home from Westcott on the bus, I sat next to a woman who had just been to Florida to visit her daughter and was on her way back to New York and her husband, who, she said, hadn't been able to eat or sleep since she'd been gone. She'd planned to stay another week, but because of him she'd had to cut it short. She had big flappy eyelids, and while she yapped to me about her husband, she flapped her lids at a marine across the aisle, and when I got off at Trilby he moved into my seat. Which a week ago I might have laughed at but now only added to the sordidness of life.

When I got home, I found Mother and Father were having the Nobles for dinner, so it would be hours before I could talk to them privately. I wasn't sorry. I felt this was some sort of omen. For the best.

"You are late," my mother said. "Studying with Bo Jo again?"

I didn't have to lie; I could just nod. She was wearing a white brocade dress cut low at the neck, and her hair was knotted in a French twist in the back. What she looked in spite of a husband, three half-grown children, and the dress, was pure. Pure and innocent.

"Run upstairs and change," my mother said. "Skirt and blouse will do but *clean.*"

My father, coming from the pantry with a tray of drinks, said, "Where have you been, my pretty maid?" He smiled at me. I didn't smile back. I didn't dare move my face in case it might start crying.

The Nobles are a jolly couple with big, round voices that crowd any room they're in. They raise racehorses and cocker spaniels and drink too many cocktails before dinner. They don't have any children of their own and are absolutely maudlin over us, which I think is kind of touching, but Gregory takes to the bed with an earache as soon as he hears they are coming. They didn't stay late. Mother and Father went with them to the door. I watched them from the sun porch where I was listening to the "Moonlight Sonata" on the stereo. Mother had her hand tucked in Father's arm, and the Nobles beamed and gushed away about what a marvelous evening and what

24

wonderful, beautiful intelligent children, and how proud they must be. . . . I felt sick to my stomach. I turned off the stereo and started up to bed. I didn't get far before Mother called to me.

"If you're not too tired," she said, "your father and I would like to talk to you a minute." For a second I thought they must be on to something . . . but her voice sounded much too relaxed for that.

We sat, the three of us, in the living room with the empty glasses and the full ashtrays and the aftertaste of Mrs. Nobles' perfume, and Mother lit a cigarette . . . she never smokes unless she's terribly nervous or terribly bored. She said, "Darling, your father and I think you are seeing entirely too much of this Bo Jo Jones."

I couldn't help thinking how simple it would be if I could, laughing raucously, tell her that that was the understatement of the year. "It's not," my father said, looking embarrassed .. he always looks embarrassed when Mother makes him come poking into our business . . . "that we've anything against the boy personally . . . hardly know him in fact . . . but you're much too lively and attractive to, to, get in a rut . . . to, to limit yourself. . . ."

"For instance," Mother said, "what has become of all your other friends? Tommy Ryan and Rodney and Julius?"

I said, "I still see them every day at school. And lots of times we all do things together Saturday night."

"But you don't actually date anyone but Bo Jo," my mother said. And it wasn't a question.

"As I said before," Father said, "it isn't that we have anything against him, but just who is he? What does his father do?"

"I don't know. Bo Jo told me, but I've forgotten. He's away a lot. Frankly, I've never met his parents, but I can assure you they're perfectly nice, respectable citizens though I don't see why that matters as long as Bo Jo is a nice, respectable citizen, which he is." I was beginning to feel boxed in, but one thing I knew for sure—I could never tell these people the truth.

"Well," my mother said, "we're not going to forbid you to go on seeing Bo Jo, but we are going to ask you not to go on seeing him so often."

"After all, it's only fair to give the other boys a fighting chance," my father said.

"I'll think about it," I said.

On my way upstairs I heard my father say, "Do you think we got anywhere?"

And my mother say, "I'm sure we did. I think she's probably already a little bored with the boy. In all the times he's been here I've never heard him say two words."

I gave Bo Jo the bad news the next day in the same booth in the same drugstore where all those million trillion years ago we had promised not to let things get out of hand again.

He didn't faint, and he didn't swear, and he didn't actually break down and cry the way I was afraid for a minute he was going to. He has brown, stubbly, non-descript hair and a stubbly nondescript nose, but there is nothing nondescript about his eyes. They are a very bright unadulterated blue, living color to be exact, but when I finished telling him they were pale, washed out, watered down like the eyes of a Weimaraner dog.

"There must be some way around it," he said.

"Anything you can name I have thought of," I said.

"There are doctors . . ."

"I know, but I can't, I simply can't. . . ."

"Scared?"

"Of course. But something else too. I simply can't, that's all. Crazy as it sounds, I simply don't believe in it. Crazy as it sounds, I think it would be wrong, I mean *really* wrong." I blew my nose and hunched down in my seat. I hadn't exactly expected hearts and flowers and a shoulder to cry on, but I was beginning to feel like I'd come to the wrong address, dialed the wrong number. . . .

"Have you told your family?"

"No."

He got up and went to the other end of the store and came back with a pack of cigarettes. "I think maybe you should, don't you?" He handed me the opened pack, but I refused, and he lit one for himself. He didn't know much about smoking and nothing about inhaling, and he looked like a teakettle at full boil.

I said, "I think you're trying to tell me something, but

26

I'd like to hear it straight if you don't mind. I think you're trying to tell me that this is *my* little red wagon. *All* mine. I think—"

"Aw no, kid!" He reached under the table and grabbed my hand. "I'm just scared like you. And studying the angles ... Look, look at me." I did, and his eyes were almost back to their normal color. "You don't really think I'd run out on you, do you?"

"I just don't know," I blubbered. For a girl who likes to cry I'd done pretty well until then. "Actually I guess there are a lot of things I don't know about you." He handed me a handkerchief. It smelled of car grease, but I used it anyhow.

"If it's marriage you want, we'll do it."

"Of course I don't *want* it!" I said. "Not any more than you do. But what else?"

He dropped my hand and stubbed out his cigarette. "You got me there," he said. "When and where do we wrap it up?"

We wrapped it up three days later on a Saturday in a town over the line in Georgia, where we'd heard they'd marry anybody sober enough to stand up and lie about their age.

It was over a hundred miles from Trilby, three hours by car and four by Bo Jo's father's truck, which was the best we could do for conveyance after Bo Jo told his father that he wanted the car for an all-day picnic. I hadn't slept much the night before. Fortunately Mother and Father went out to dinner. I don't think I could have got through the last supper bit. Grace and Gregory and I ate spaghetti in the kitchen, and afterwards I played Monopoly with "Gory." That's my special name for him because he hates Gregory. Everyone thinks it's divine and won't call him anything else. It's made a kind of a bond between us. We both also like collecting small wild animals, like birds and squirrels, and making pets of them. He's only twelve, but he has some pretty long thoughts about things and wants to be a medical missionary when he grows up and go and live in Thailand, if it's still around. Actually I feel much closer to him as a human being than I do to anyone else in the family. Because I didn't know how long it would be before I played Monopoly with him again, I let him win. Instead of jumping up and down and crowing like I expected him to, he said, "What's the matter with you? You've been acting awful funny lately."

He pushed back his chair and scowled at me. He looked just like Father when he's about to go meddling in our business, embarrassed, only unlike Father, his ears stick out and his hair stands straight up in front on account of a cowlick.

"Nothing's the matter," I said.

"You act like you're in love or something," he said.

I turned this over in my mind. Here was an opening, a chance to tell him something he could look back to later and know I'd not really deceived him, something to lessen tomorrow's shock a little.

"Maybe I am," I said.

"I guess there's always a first time," he said. "Wanta play another game?"

"It's past your bedtime."

"I know." He began dividing out the play money, and we shook for first turn.

"Is it Bo Jo Jones?" He was still scowling, not really concentrating on the Monopoly game at all. I nodded.

"Mother and Father don't like him."

"They don't know him."

"I know. I tried to tell them what a great football guy he is. Sammy Greene's father played football at State U, and he says he'll send Bo Jo there with his own money if he can't make it any other way. . . ."

"Bo Jo doesn't need his money. He's already got a scholarship," I said.

"Gee, that's great. You and him going steady?"

"Real steady."

"Can I tell? Can I tell Sammy Greene?"

"If you like."

"You know"—again he leaned back, the game all but forgotten—"boys my age aren't supposed to like girls, but I do. What I mean is I don't see anything wrong with them and there's this one girl sits next to me in assembly that smells of soap. Some kind of soap. If I ever take a girl to the movies, that's who I'll take."

"Is she pretty?"

"Naw." He yawned. Already bored with the subject.

"It's up to bed with you," I said. "You're only pretending to play Monopoly and not even doing that very well."

"O.K., O.K., don't rush me." He stretched, yawned again, got up and walked stiff and bent over in imtiation of an old man to the door. At the door he held a forefinger to his forehead. "Pow!" he said, and spinning from the impact of his imaginary bullet, crumpled to the floor.

"Oh, go on with you! Quit your stalling!" I said, but suddenly there was a lump in my throat. By tomorrow night at this time everything would be changed between us and never the same again.

Grace helped me do the dishes, which was real square of her, as I was supposedly baby-sitting and being paid for it, which included the dishes. She was down in the dumps about an English test, which she was sure she'd flunked, and I envied her with all my heart. I guess more than anything I was beginning to miss the trivialities of life.

"The trouble is I can read a thing," Grace said, "and actually enjoy it, but two days later I can't remember the names of the characters much less what the allegory was supposed to be."

"Such as?"

"At least a quarter of the test today was on Conrad."

"I don't think girls should have to read Conrad ... unless they want to."

"You don't?"

"Actually I think English should be divided into girls and boys. English at least until you get to high school. What boy wants to read *Jane Eyre*—"

"I adore that," Grace broke in. "I could tell you the name of everyone in it!"

"That's just what I mean, but you won't find any English teacher quizzing a class of boys on the Brontë sisters."

"I never thought of that. Gee, maybe you should be a teacher. Have you thought yet about what you want to be?"

For a minute I couldn't answer. I felt as though I'd been hit in the solar plexus and had the wind knocked out of me. No, I hadn't thought much about it, and now it

29

was too late. I didn't have any choice anymore. What I wanted to be and what I would be no longer had any relation one to the other.

"I don't think you're listening," Grace said. "You look like your mind is a hundred miles away."

"I've always been interested in plays, you know that," I said crossly. "Acting them, writing them . . ." Those days, those dreams, seemed years ago.

"You're so lucky," Grace said, "to have something you are truly interested in. I used to have lots of interests," she sighed, "making doll's clothes, having tea parties in the tree house . . . but they don't interest me now. Naturally. I'm not a little girl anymore. But I'm not a big girl either." She sighed again. "What did you do in-between, July?"

I tried to remember, but it didn't seem to me that there'd been any in-between. But then I'd never played dolls or had tea parties in the tree house. My idea of good times was centered around Holly Hill, Grandmother Greher's place in the country, picking berries, climbing trees, putting on plays in the old carriage house with Tilda Green's six children and Grandmother Greher's hunting dogs as our only audience. I can't remember that I ever outgrew the place and the things we did there; it was simply that other sorts of things began crowding in, and before I knew it, there just wasn't time anymore.

"I can't remember what I did," I told Grace, "but I wouldn't wory about it if I were you. You've got school and Beta Club and oodles of friends." As I ticked off all the things she had to do with her young and carefree days, I started feeling sorry for myself again. "Really, Grace," I said, "I'd count my blessings if I were you and not go around crying little-girl tears about wanting to be a big girl. You'll be one soon enough!"

"But I'm NOT crying. I was just asking. A simple question. Why do you always have to fuss at me about everything!" She threw down her dish towel and stomped out. This was more like our usual relationship and somehow made me feel better. I didn't mind finishing the dishes alone. They were pretty dishes, a blue and rose pattern on an ivory background. I'd grown quite attached to them over the years and that night handled them with special care.

Mary Ann called about ten. She was baby-sitting with the "orphans" and they were all in bed and asleep. She had just had a letter from Alan—that's the boy she's pinned to—and in it he asked her if she could find a date for a friend of his for spring house party weekend. That's the big thing at Bowers, the biggest social blow of the year, in fact, and any girl would give her eyeteeth to get an invite. This boy was from Buenos Aires, his father being a professor of English literature at the university there, and that is why the boy didn't know any girl he could ask. Alan said that this boy was considered real "in" on campus and that just not any girl would fit the situation. Alan said—and Mary Ann read it to me from the letter—"How about your redhead friend, the one who likes long-haired music and short-haired men?" Mary Ann said, "I know you're all for Bo Jo Jones right now, but spring house party isn't for weeks, and anything can happen between now and then.

I said, "I appreciate the thought, but I don't think Bo Jo would want me to."

There was a minute's silence, and then Mary Ann said, "Oh, so it's like that between you."

I said, "More or less."

"I still think you should think it over. As I said, it's a long way off and this is a real opportunity to broaden your outlook."

All my life I'd wanted to go to a Bowers spring house party. Who didn't? "It may be a long way off," I said, "but it's right now I have to say yes or no, so I'm saying no."

"You really are all gone on the guy, aren't you?"

I was upset about the date with the boy from Buenos Aires, which I could never have, and by something in Mary Ann's voice, that I couldn't quite analyze. "I don't think you like Bo Jo," I said.

"Why, sure, I like him. I think he's real cute. In fact, I know a number of people . . . naming no names . . . who'd give half of Georgia to be in your shoes . . . but I just can't visualize the two of you. I mean, what do you have in common?"

"I love to watch football," I said, "and we both like to dance."

"But what do you *talk* about?" Mary Ann said.

"Goodness, what difference does *that* make! It so happens that Bo Jo is a very reserved type. It is one of the things I like about him."

"Don't get mad. I was only asking. You've been so touchy lately I never know what to say ... and I don't feel as though I ever see you anymore. When I got this letter from Alan, I thought it would be so great. I could hardly wait to get to the phone."

"I'm sorry," I murmured.

"Not nearly as sorry as I am. You know how far ahead of myself I get. I already had this guy flipping over you, and you and I going up to Bowers together every other weekend. ... Remember what fun we had the time my uncle had us up to State U for Class Day? Well, this would have been that all over again and then some. Besides, I want you and Alan to get to know each other. He's such a wonderful guy when you get to know him. Real deep. And as my best friend, you'll undoubtedly be seeing a lot of each other in the future, and it's important to me that you get to be friends. ..."

Of course, she had no way of knowing how miserable she was making me. I simply couldn't stand any more. I held the receiver off from my ear until her voice stopped coming out of it, and then I hung up. It was a nasty, childish thing to do, but by tomorrow or the day after, she was bound to understand.

When Mother and Father came in around midnight, I pretended to be asleep. They came into my room, and Mother shut one of the windows and Father pulled up the blanket over my shoulders, and then they went out and down the hall to Grace's room. I wondered where I'd be tomorrow night at this time. Bo Jo said he thought we ought to spend the night at a motel and call our folks from there in case they tried to get the marriage annulled on the grounds that it hadn't been consummated. But I pointed out that we had proof that it had if worse came to worse, and I didn't think it would be fair to tell them on the telephone. Bo Jo said he guessed it would be kind of chicken but that frankly he was feeling chicken. And if we

32

his wife to come in and witness the ceremony. I don't even remember what she looked like or what kind of prayer book he read from. It could have been Mohammedan. It certainly didn't sound like any marriage service I'd ever heard before, but then my ears were ringing so it was hard to tell.

We were married with the same dime store ring I'd bought in Westcott to fool the doctor with.

When it was over, his wife said, "Well, aren't you going to kiss the bride?" For a minute I thought she was talking to her husband, so I backed off, but it was Bo Jo she meant. He kissed me on the cheek. By that time we were both ravenous with hunger and went to a Howard Johnson, where Bo Jo had three hamburgers and a banana split, and I had one hamburger and two chocolate malteds. When we got back in the truck, Bo Jo counted his money. He figured he had enough for gas back to Trilby and eight bucks over. He said, "I'll be back in a minute." There was a florist shop across the street and he went into it. When I saw him come out with a small purple box in his hand, I got a lump in my throat as big as a grapefruit. He put the box on the seat between us, and I opened it. It was a white orchid tied with a white ribbon.

"I would have got it before," he said, "but I had to see how much that marriage merchant was going to charge first."

I didn't say anything because I couldn't. The grapefruit was in the way. But Bo Jo got the picture. He grinned and pinned the orchid onto my collar, where it scratched my chin and made it hard to move my head.

We didn't talk much on the way home. I guess we were pretty busy with our own thoughts. I began to wish that I hadn't scotched his idea of a long-distance call to our parents from a motel, and if I hadn't known how broke he was, I would have said so. I noticed too that the closer we got to home, the slower he drove.

Finally when we stopped at a filling station for gas, he said, "You can do whatever you want about your family, but I'm calling mine. Now. From here. Pop's got a temper like a meat ax, and Ma is going to cry for a solid week. I want to give them a head start." He didn't wait for me to

37

answer. He was already out of the car before I could get my breath.

I went into the rest room and washed my face and combed my hair and put on fresh lipstick. I dragged it out, but Bo Jo still hadn't got through with his call. I could see him through the big plate glass window of the filling station. The phone was against the wall on the right as you went in, and not very high up. His forehead leaned against his hand, which was crooked over the top of the phone, and with his other hand he held the receiver against his ear and his ear, even from where I was, looked very red. He didn't seem to be saying much. Mostly listening. I went and got in the truck. My back and head were beginning to ache from riding so much, and the white orchid was beginning to turn brown at the edges. Finally, after what seemed like ages, Bo Jo came out and got in the driver's seat. He looked beat, and his ears weren't red anymore—they were white like the rest of his face, which looked as though it had been dunked in some kind of a bleach. I couldn't think of anything to say that was fitting, so I didn't say anything. He started the car.

"Well, that's settled," he said. "You won't have to stay with my folks." He made like a laugh.

"Meaning?"

"Meaning we aren't wanted. To say the least. Meaning that I am, as of now, on my own." He laughed again in an unfunny way. "I was their great white hope, see? My son the college boy! And now I'm nothing but a seventeen-year-old punk with a wife, and so it's quits between us. Just like that! Jesus, I thought I meant something. Me. Their kid. But the first time I'm in trouble, the very first time . . ."

"Maybe if you'd told them in person," I said.

"Boy, am I glad I didn't! You know, I actually think Pop would have taken a strap to me. If he could have got his hands on me, I actually think he would have taken a strap. . . ."

"But you knew he'd be mad. You expected it. You said he had a temper so maybe that's all it is, is his temper." Frankly, I was glad we couldn't go to his house, but I hated to see him so hurt about it. I couldn't imagine my parents acting like that, and if they did, well, I'd just die.

38

"Look, don't try smoothing things over," Bo Jo said. "You won't get me near that place again. Not in a million years." I didn't say anything, and pretty soon he said, "I'll have to take him back his damned truck."

"Just what did happen?" I said. "What did you tell them?"

"I gave it to them straight," Bo Jo said. "I told them I was married."

"No lead-up?"

"How the hell do you lead up to a thing like that?"

"I don't know. I sort of thought I'd start by telling Mother and Father how much I love them and how I hate to let them down, et cetera . . ."

"That's a woman for you!" Bo Jo snorted.

"Well, it's the truth! I do love them, and I do hate to . . ." We passed a road sign that said TRILBY, 25 MILES.

"Are you going to tell them about the baby?" Bo Jo said.

"Of course not."

"Then how'll you explain it?"

"I will tell them I'm madly in love. They'll find out about the baby soon enough. Did you tell your family?"

"They didn't give me a chance to. But what the hell, they know. They know I'd never . . ." He stopped. Just in time, I'm sure. Because that would have been the last straw. The very last. I took the orchid off and put it back in its box. I told him it was because if I walked in from a picnic wearing an orchid my parents would know something was screwy, but actually it was because it was beginning to lose its meaning. I also took off the heels and put on sandals, likewise the pearls and earrings.

It was fresh dark when we drove up in front of my house. I mean, you could still see things, but there were lights on in the house. It looked big and warm and happy, and I was glad it was there no matter what. I felt sorry for Bo Jo because I imagined his thoughts were quite the opposite.

I said, "You don't absolutely have to come in with me. You could ride around awhile, until . . . I could tell them that you're breaking it to your folks . . . Hey," I said, "you don't suppose your folks called mine or anything like that? That would be *terrible!*"

"Worry not," Bo Jo said, "my folks don't know your name."

"They don't?"

"They didn't ask."

"They didn't ask who you'd married?" I was truly shocked. And humiliated, and I simply couldn't understand the type of people Bo Jo's parents must be.

"Oh, they know I've ben dating you a lot. Not by name but by that picture you gave me, so I guess they figure that's who I married. Anyhow they didn't ask. They had too much else on their minds."

"Well, as I was saying," I said, "you don't have to come in with me." I guess I sounded kind of cold and distant, because Bo Jo put his arm around me. Actually it was the first time he'd put his arm around me in days, and it almost broke me up.

"Come off it, kid," he said. "I'm chicken all right, but not *that* chicken. Pin a smile on and let's get it over."

I pinned a smile on, and we walked up the path holding hands. "Quite a mansion," Bo Jo said. The house we live in is large and ugly and oldish and in the part of town where all the houses are large and ugly and oldish with high ceilings and lots of halls and all kinds of waste space. Grandmother Greher gave it to Father and Mother for a wedding present for which Mother has never quite forgiven her, but it was a marvelous house for hide-and-seek when we were little, and a good house for going your own way in now that we're older, but I'd never thought of it as especially grand.

"It needs paint," I said, "and a new kitchen."

"My mother wouldn't be caught dead in it," he said, "but it's got class. You've got to hand it that."

We walked up the steps and in the door and down the hall to the living room. Upstairs Grace had the record player in her room on full blast—Bobby Darin singing some icky "why don't you love me" song, and off to the right on the sun porch Gory was playing ping-pong with somebody—*crack, plop, crack*. Bo Jo let my hand go, and I walked into the living room. Father was there reading the paper. Bo Jo stayed in the doorway waiting, I guess, for an invite.

I said, "Hi."

40

Father said, "Mmmm" without looking up.

I said, "Where's Mother?"

He said, "In the pantry making canapes; we're having a few people in for drinks."

I said, "Oh," and he finally looked up and said, "How was the picnic?" and saw Bo Jo sort of lingering in the doorway and said, "Come in, boy, come in." And went back to his paper.

I gave Bo Jo a look that tried to say "Don't mind him," but Bo Jo stayed put, so I said, "Let's go and find Mother."

He followed me into the pantry. Mother was spreading something on crackers. "Hello there," she said. "So you decided not to go dancing?"

"Something like that," I said.

"How are you this evening, Mrs. Greher?" Bo Jo said.

"Oh, hello, Bo Jo," my mother said. "I think this needs something, but I don't know what." She handed each of us a spread cracker. I tasted mine.

"Salt," I said. "Are you having many people?"

"Just the Hammells and the Clarks and their nephew from San Francisco. I'm glad you're back. He's a little old for you, twenty, but he's much too young for us certainly. Perhaps you could take him over to the club for a while."

"Mother," I said, "I happen to have a date with Bo Jo tonight."

"I meant Bo Jo too, of course." She gave Bo Jo one of her coaxing smiles, but he wasn't looking.

"I don't belong to the club," Bo Jo said.

"You'd go as July's guest, of course," my mother said.

"We sort of wanted to stay home tonight," I said. I took a deep breath. "We wanted to talk to you and Father about something."

"Oh, dear, I *am* sorry," Mother said, and shook some salt into the spread and tasted it. "Perhaps tomorrow. Your father has a golf date in the morning but by afternoon . . ."

"But this is important," I said.

"Maybe these people won't stay too long," my mother said.

"Are they staying for supper?" I said.

"Oh, no. Just cocktails." Mother gave Bo Jo another

smile just like the one that hadn't taken. "So why don't you two take this nephew off somewhere, and then when they leave we can have our talk?"

"Look," Bo Jo said to me, "I think I'll mosey down to the Coffee Pot. Whyn't you call me there later?"

"But . . ." I said, and didn't know where to go from there. But what? Stick around and help me entertain San Francisco? Tell them all to go to the devil and take me with you?

"Oh dear," Mother said, "I didn't mean to interfere with your date. I just thought . . ."

"See you later," Bo Jo said.

I went to the door with him, but I didn't get a chance to say anything to him. The Hammells and the Clarks and the nephew were coming up the front steps.

The nephew turned out to be a perfect dream boat of a guy in spite of his name, which was Horace, and his wavy blond hair, which made him look more like Dr. Kildare than Dr. Kildare does.

We stayed in the living room with the others, but at the far end where we could talk without having to scream above the cackling and gay, gay laughter of the older people. His voice was a little on the high twangy side, but that was because he came from the Midwest originally, and once I got used to it it wasn't too bad. He seemed a little disappointed when he found out I was only a junior in high school.

"You look older than that," he said, "or maybe I should say wiser." He himself was a sophomore at Stanford and planning to transfer to Princeton next year. A vision of Princeton weekends, like sugar plums, danced through my head, but only fleetingly.

"What are your interests?" he was saying to me.

"In what line?"

"Let's start with music and build from there." He had a nice smile, but it only went halfway, as though he were afraid to unloose it all over his face.

"I gather that's your big interest," I said.

"Madrigals, ballads . . . the zither . . . a guitar leaves me cold."

"How odd, why?"

"It swallows up the lyrics and drowns the melody. . . .

"I beg to differ."

"But the fiddle . . . ah, the fiddle . . ." He tilted back his head and pretended to be listening.

"Do you ever try composing?"

He blushed. "How did you know that? How on earth did you know that?" He looked at me as though I were some sort of magic.

"My crystal ball," I said. The truth was it had been my experience that anybody real gone on folk music is always trying to make up something on their own. Even I wrote some lyrics once . . . the title of the song was "The Boy with the Patches and the Girl in Blue," but whenever I tried to find a tune to fit it, I came up with "On Top of Old Smoky."

"I really think you come through to me," he said. "E.S.P. is what it is. I've a drawerful of rejects, but I've about quit. I am now taking up skin diving. Have you ever seen a coral reef underwater?"

"Yes, once off the coast of Florida . . ."

"And what do you think of Salinger?"

"I accept him. I accept him all the way."

"How about D. H. Lawrence?"

"Who's he?"

"I can't wait to tell you . . . but I guess I'll have to . . . wait until you grow up." He was looking at me fondly as though he considered me some sort of new discovery that he intended to go on with indefinitely, and I realized to my horror that I hadn't even thought of Bo Jo once nor remembered about being married. "In the meantime, will you write to me?"

I looked at him blankly.

"If I write to you, of course."

"I'll try," I said stupidly, thinking now of Bo Jo, of being married.

"What do you mean you'll try?" He grinned. "What's the address?"

I gave it to him. I didn't know what else to do. It was after nine when they left. I rushed to the phone to call Bo Jo, but Mother waylaid me in the hall.

"Darling," she said, "do you really think this is a very good time for important talks? Can't it wait until tomorrow?"

43

I was about to say it couldn't possibly when Father, coming out of the living room with a tray of empty glasses, said, "Can't what wait?"

"Bo Jo," Mother said. "He has something he wants to talk to us about."

"Not he. We," I said.

"Sounds ominous," Father said, and grinned. "Don't tell me you want to ask permission to go steady. And I thought the age of chivalry was dead!"

"Nothing as childish as that," I said.

"Anything less childish is out," my father said. "Absolutely out."

I could feel myself getting cold and clammy, and my hands were shaking. Mother must have noticed because she said, "Darling, what is it? You look positively ill."

"I'm not," I said. "I'm married." Just like that. No lead-up. No soft-pedal. Just the crescendo and me starting to bawl.

They led me into Father's study and sat me down in the squooshiest chair and shut the door.

"She can't really be," Father said. "Nobody would marry them. . . ."

"But you heard her. She said she was. . . ."

"She's hysterical. Didn't mean it, I'm sure. Impossible!"

"Then why is she hysterical?"

"Where's the instigator of all this hullabaloo?" Father roared. "Where has he run off to?"

"He hasn't run off anywhere," I said. "He's at the Coffee Pot waiting for me to call him so we could tell you together. Only I . . ."

"Tell us what?" my father said in an "I dare you" voice.

"That we're married."

"How can you be?" my father said. "You're only sixteen."

"There's this place in Georgia."

"But why? Why, why, why?" My mother walked over to the window. Her back was to me, but I could see her shoulders shaking and even though she didn't make any crying noise, I knew that she was crying.

"I still don't believe it," my father said, walking up and down in front of the squooshie chair and looking at me

44

from time to time as though I were some new specimen of creature heretofore unknown. "You wouldn't do a damned fool thing like that. A bloody cruel thing like that. Knock the pops right out from under us. Throw your life away. Not that we'll let you. These things can always be annulled—Agnes, Agnes, did you hear me? We'll have it annulled. Should be simple. They're both under age. They didn't have our permission, they . . ."

"I'm going to call Bo Jo," I said, and got up out of the squooshie chair.

"Bo Jo!" The way my father said it, it sounded like a swear word.

"Paul," my mother said, still with her back to us. "Please keep your voice down. I don't want the children to hear. . . ."

"His name," I said, "is Boswell Johnson Jones, and I happen to be very much in love with him."

"What in heaven's name," my father said, "can you possibly know about love?"

"I'm going to call Bo Jo," I said again. It was now almost ten o'clock.

"By all means," my father said. "I want to talk to him. I most certainly want to talk to him."

"Where did we fail her?" my mother said. "What did we ever do to make her want to hurt us?"

She turned around then, and her eyes were all streaky with crying, and her mouth didn't seem to have any shape to it. "Is it because your father and I disapproved of your seeing so much of this boy? Is that why you've done this to us?"

"Of course it isn't," I said, and went out into the hall and called the Coffee Pot. I asked if Bo Jo Jones was there. I said he was wearing a madras jacket and had blue eyes. The man at the other end said he'd see. He came back in a few minutes and said somebody answering that description had been there but he'd left. I went back in the living room and told Mother and Father that he wasn't there.

"Wasn't where?" Father said.

"At the Coffee Pot."

"Then call his home. The sooner we get this settled and done with . . ."

45

"He won't be at home. His father kicked him out."

Mother, who was looking out the window again, said, "There's a truck parked at the curb and someone in it."

"He probably ran out of change for coffee," I said, and went and looked out of the window. It was Bo Jo all right. My father started out of the room, but I caught up with him and grabbed his hand.

"Please," I said, "let me." And for some reason he did. I think Bo Jo was asleep, but he wouldn't admit it.

He said, "Look, maybe we ought to save the bad news for tomorrow. It's late, and your folks are probably pooped."

"It is, and they are, but I've already told them. They want to see you."

"That's a switch."

"They think I did it just to hurt them. Deliberately. Mother's been reading Jung or maybe it's Adler."

He got out of the car, and we walked up to the house.

"They want it annulled," I said.

"I figured that would be the first angle," Bo Jo said. "I knew we should have stayed at a motel."

"Maybe we still can," I said.

"I'm fresh out of rent."

"I've got fifteen dollars I was saving for a new stereo."

"We'll see how things ride with them," Bo Jo said. "I'd planned to sack out in the truck for tonight."

"And tomorrow?"

"Maybe if we don't look, tomorrow will go away," Bo Jo said.

Mother and Father weren't in the study. They'd moved to the living room, and the minute we walked in I knew that they'd been putting two and two together and had come up with four. The whole atmosphere was distinctly different. The hysterics had gone out of the air, but it was heavier and sadder, and I found myself wishing that they were like Bo Jo's folks and would just scream and yell and kick us out. Mother sat in a corner of the sofa with her feet huddled under her as though they were cold; Father sat on the arm of the sofa beside her. I don't know which one looked more beat.

"Sit down," Father said.

I sat in the low-backed rocker where I always sit when

I'm nervous, and Bo Jo sat in the first chair he came to, which was unfortunately Father's favorite, and no one ever sat in it if Father was in the room.

"Your mother and I have been talking this over, and there are a few questions we want to ask you. . . ."

"Only one," my mother said in a shaking voice.

"Whatever your answer," my father said, "we are agreed that an annulment is still the only solution, but this would admittedly complicate things." He stopped and glared at Bo Jo.

"Yes, sir," Bo Jo said.

"Then you do know what I'm driving at?"

Bo Jo looked at me, and I said, "What are you driving at, Father?"

"Have I got to put it in words?" Father said, and looked at Mother, who looked at her hands, which were holding each other in her lap and said, "Are you two in trouble, July?"

I started to speak, but Bo Jo straightened up in Father's chair and leaned forward. I didn't say anything, and after a minute of leaning forward and cracking his knuckles, he said, "We were, Mrs. Greher. We aren't anymore." I could have kissed him. I could have jumped up and down and clapped my hands. I thought, That's your husband talking—and it was a proud thought.

"What do you mean, not anymore?" my father said. "Don't tell me you got rid—"

"Don't!" I said. "Don't talk about it that way. Don't make it ugly and sordid because it isn't." I began rocking furiously, and I could feel tears running down my face, though I didn't knew where they came from.

"She's tired," Bo Jo said. "Why don't you let her go to bed?"

"I think we could all do with some sleep," my mother said. "Things always look different in the morning."

"There's just one thing that has me confused," I said. "What did Father mean about how this would *complicate* getting an annulment? I should think it would absolutely close the subject."

"Not if you plan to have the baby adopted," Mother said.

"But that's the point, we don't," I said.

"Just what do you plan?" Father said. "To put Bo Jo in our guest room and when the baby comes, give it yours?" I had no idea my father had such a bitter sense of humor.

"I'm going to get a job," Bo Jo said. "I already have one job Saturdays. I figure that with another after school we can scrape by." He got up out of Father's chair, and suddenly I couldn't stand the idea of being left here alone with them.

"Wait for me," I said to Bo Jo. I went upstairs and packed an overnight bag and got the fifteen dollars out of my jewel case. When I came down, my parents were waiting at the foot of the stairs.

Father said, "Please stay here tonight. I'm sorry if we hurt you, but you've hurt us. You belong here, July. Here with your parents . . ."

"We only want to take care of you," Mother said, "to protect you . . ."

"To do what's best," Father said.

"But we've already decided what's best," I said, and tried to edge past them to where Bo Jo waited for me in the doorway.

"Bo Jo can stay here. In . . . in Gory's room," Mother said.

"I'm scared to stay here," I said. I was. I was scared if I did I might end up doing what they wanted. Right now they seemed more real than Bo Jo or myself or this invisible seed that was going to grow into a baby. And bigger and stronger, and by tomorrow I would probably remember too how much I loved them. "I've got to go," I said out loud.

"But if you do, the whole town will know," my father said.

"It will all be settled," my mother said. "Please don't do this to us. To yourself."

"You are breaking your mother's heart," Father said.

"What do you think's happening to hers?" Bo Jo said. "Come on, kid if you're coming." It was what I needed to get me past Mother's stretched-out hands and Father's eyes.

"Where will you stay?" Father said.

"At the Twilight Motel," Bo Jo said.

"Make it the Inn," Father said. "At least do that much

48

for us." He shoved a twenty-dollar bill into the pocket of Bo Jo's jacket.

"And, and, call me in the morning," Mother said, "as soon as you wake up."

It was embarrassing at the Inn. We had to show them our marriage license, and when it came to writing down our address Bo Jo took so long the clerk said, "What's the matter, buddy, can't make up your mind?" However, the room made up for it with big red chintz roses hanging at the windows and wall-to-wall carpeting you could dig your feet into. By the time I'd bathed, Bo Jo was asleep. I had expected to lie awake crying all night, but the minute my head hit the pillow I was out like a light.

When I woke up it was because the sun was in my eyes, and Bo Jo was thumping around in the shower. The whole place smelled of soap and spring air, and in a minute he came steaming out of the bathroom with a towel wrapped around his waist. It's a funny thing about clothes or the lack of them. This towel covered a lot more of Bo Jo than his bathing trunks do, but because it wasn't bathing trunks but a towel I felt uncomfortable. I mean I wasn't accustomed to a man walking around in my bedroom with practically nothing on.

"You sleep with your mouth open," Bo Jo said, and came and sat down on the side of my bed. His hair was still wet from the shower, and it spiked up here and there like new baby horns, and his eyes were bluer than I remembered. I guess that was because I'd never seen them so early in the day before.

"How revolting," I said. "Do I really?"

"I should have said with your lips parted." Bo Jo grinned. "Sounds better."

"I think it's cruel to spy on people in their sleep."

"I wasn't spying," Bo Jo said. "I was just taking inventory. Move over."

I moved over, and Bo Jo flicked the towel off and got in beside me. "This doesn't all have to be downbeat, does it, kid?" He scooped my shoulders into the crook of his arm. "There's more to this married bit than grief and sorrow. Remember?"

The truth was I hardly did. I felt strange and shy. I

49

suppose it was the sunlight. Before, it had been dark. And the room. Before, there had been the sky to look at.

"Race you dressed," Bo Jo said.

"But I don't want to get dressed," I said. "I want breakfast in bed."

"You mean lunch," Bo Jo said.

"What I mean is scrambled eggs and bacon and sausage and grits and toast, whatever time it is."

"I've never had breakfast in bed," Bo Jo said. "How's it done?"

"Well, first you order. On the telephone. And then you languish until it comes. When Mother and Father took me to New York to absorb culture I had breakfast in bed every morning."

"Does it cost more that way?"

"Lots more."

"Well, we haven't got lots more," Bo Jo said. "Know what this room cost?"

"Money, money, always money." I sat up and swung my legs over the side of the bed. "Oh well, the Coffee Pot has divine doughnuts."

"You can come back here and languish afterwards," Bo Jo said. "It's all ours until five P.M."

"Until five P.M.," I said. "Just like Cinderella. Only what do we turn back into at five P.M.?"

"Two jobless, homeless kids who had to get married," Bo Jo said. "But you know, for a little while there I forgot. I completely forgot."

"So did I," I said.

We looked at each other and smiled. And then Bo Jo picked up his towel off the floor and went into the bathroom.

The telephone rang just as we were about to leave the room. It was Mother. She said they were putting Sunday dinner on the table and why didn't we come and have some? Hungry as I was, I wasn't ready to face reality again. Or them. I wanted to go on with the Cinderella game until the clock struck five. I wanted to go to the Coffee Pot with Bo Jo and then come back to this room and write a letter to someone on the Inn stationery. I didn't know who. Just anyone.

50

I said, "Thank you, Mother, and don't think we don't appreciate the thought, but we've already eaten." I was shocked at how easily the lie slid out. Just as though I'd been doing it all my life, which I certainly hadn't.

"Where did you eat?" Mother sounded worried.

"At the Coffee Pot."

"Did you run into anyone you know?"

"No."

"That's a blessing. We must get things settled before you do. Make our plans. I mean your plans. When *are* we going to see you?"

I put my hand over the receiver and asked Bo Jo when we were going to see them. He said, "That's up to you."

I said, "Later on this afternoon."

"Are you all right?" Mother said with a catch in her voice.

"Fine."

"Well, we'll be waiting. You do understand how important it is that we get together as soon as possible?"

"Yes. And Mother, thank Father for the, the Inn."

"He's right here. Do you want to speak to him?"

"I'll see you both later," I said, because I honestly didn't know what to say to him. We had both changed so much since day before yesterday.

At the Coffee Pot we sat at the counter because we could get served faster there, and the only chance we had to talk was when the man behind the counter was waiting on someone else or yelling orders through a hole in the wall to the cook.

"I've been thinking," Bo Jo said. "This is no time to be . . ."

"Do you like your bacon well done or . . ." the man said.

"Or," Bo Jo said.

"No time to be proud," Bo Jo said. "And the thing to do, the thing I'm going to do, what I've got to do, in fact, having no choice . . ."

"Hey sonny, I bet you're the guy some dame was calling here last night. Name of Bo Jo?" the man said.

"Could be."

"Having no choice," Bo Jo said, "I'm going around and give my folks a chance to say they didn't mean it."

"Do you think maybe they didn't?"

"They've had time to simmer down," Bo Jo said. "Anyhow, that's plan A."

"And what's plan B?"

"One night," the man said, "I had this here fella whose wife kept calling ... O.K, O.K., coming up with ham on rye ... finally I put him on the phone, told him to do his own lying, and you know what he told her? ... I said on rye! ... Told her to go chase herself. He got home and found all the neighbors out trying to catch her. She was running around and around the block in her nightgown."

"Plan B," Bo Jo said, "is that we move in with them."

"But I don't even know them," I said. "I mean I'd sort of hoped ..."

"That we'd move in with *your* folks? Not in a million—"

"I guess I sort of thought that once you got a job we could get a place of our own."

"Get your head out of the clouds, kid," Bo Jo said. "What kind of job do you think I can get after school that'd pay for our own place?"

"I guess I forgot about school," I said.

"Is that what you want me to do? Forget about school?" At that exact time I guess that is just what I wanted him to do. I mean if it was that or go and live on the other side of town with some people I'd never even met, who were mad at me to start with. "Just drop the whole thing," Bo Jo said. "Spend the rest of my life carrying bags at the supermarket?"

"Not the rest of your life," I said.

"That will be two dollars and thirty-five cents," the man said.

We decided it was smarter for Bo Jo to see his folks by himself. I went back to the Inn, but I'd lost interest in writing on the Inn stationery. I'd lost interest in just about everything. I bought a paperback mystery at the desk. It cost fifty cents, but I didn't think about that. I wasn't in the habit of thinking about small change. I lay down on the bed and read. It was a lousy story, gruesome really, but it got me away for a while, and when Bo Jo walked in, it took me a minute to remember what he was doing there.

He was hot and sweaty and looked as though he might have been crying. "Well, we're all set," he said, and flopped down on a chair. "Ma's fixing up the girls' room. All we got to do is check out of here and move in."

I was beginning to feel the way I had the summer before when Mother and Father had talked about sending me north to boarding school. Furious. And trapped.

"We've got to go and see my family first," I said.

"Your family is going to raise hell," Bo Jo said. "And I've had just about all the hell I can take for one afternoon."

"Was it bad at your house?"

"Morbid. They weren't mad anymore. It was terrible."

"What were they?"

"Resigned. Beat. I told you they'd pinned everything on me. Their bagful of dreams. That was me. *Pffft!* No more dreams. I felt like I'd walked off with their life savings."

The telephone rang. It was Mother. She said, "Darling, we've waited all afternoon. Wheer are you?"

"We'll be right over," I said, "as soon as we check out."

"Please hurry," Mother said. "This has been a ghastly day for all of us." As though the minute we got there everything would stop being ghastly.

"Have you told Grace and Gory?" I said.

"I had to, but nothing definite. We sent them over to Grandmother Greher's right after dinner so when you came we could talk, but they'll be back any time now."

I hung up and Bo Jo said, "Why didn't you tell her we're going to stay with my folks?"

"Because maybe they'll have a better idea," I said, "and please if they do at least listen."

"You weren't buying their ideas last night." Bo Jo's ears were getting red.

"I'm still not buying the annulment bit," I said, "but I think they've given up on that. They were just shook last night."

"Just don't let me down," Bo Jo said. "Just don't sell me short."

I said that of course I wouldn't.

It was warm even for April so we sat on the side porch.

Or Bo Jo and Mother and I sat; Father was still pacing. Mother looked tense and harassed. Father looked bewildered and sad. We all had glasses of iced tea, which no one was drinking. Mother said, "We have had a talk with Reverend Michael, and he thinks we should let you go through with this . . . this present plan of yours. He will marry you, quietly, in the chapel tomorrow morning."

"But we already are. . . ." I said.

"A proper marriage," Mother said. "And afterwards we will send announcements to our friends and the paper. We want to preserve some remnant of dignity."

"It won't fool anybody," I said, "but if that's what you want."

"Of course it's what we want," Father said. "And I should think you'd want it too. A decent wedding, something to remember without shame."

I thought of the orchid Bo Jo had got me, of the room at the Inn this morning, the sunlight on the red chintz roses. It wasn't my shame they were talking about, it was theirs. So I said, "Yes, Father, that will be very nice."

I looked at Bo Jo, but he wasn't looking at anybody. He'd begun to drink his iced tea in great big gulps.

"Now, about the financing of this, this . . ." Father said, and stopped as though he couldn't remember what the word was.

"Marriage," I said.

"As you may or may not know," Father said to Bo Jo, "our bank is a small one, and we aren't in the habit of taking on inexperienced youths even as cashiers. Most of our people have been with us since my father's time, and the only openings have come about when someone has died or retired, but in this case we shall have to make an exception. The salary is small, but more than you can expect to get anywhere else with your lack of education and experience. It will enable you to be independent to a degree and after, after . . ."

He stopped again, and Mother said, "When the baby comes, we shall see. Reevaluate. Decide if you want to continue together. . . ."

"What are the hours?" Bo Jo said.

"Nine to five," my father said, "though at the end of the month you will have to put in some evenings too."

"I appreciate the offer," Bo Jo said, "but I can't take you up on it."

They looked at him as though he'd lost his mind. When Father got his breath, he said. "I hardly think this is a time for pride. All I'm giving you when you come right down to it is an opportunity. An opportunity to prove yourself. You may be sure if you're not capable, you'll be fired quick as the next. . . ."

"It's not that," Bo Jo said. "I wouldn't be able to go to school. There's only one more quarter, and I've got to finish it or I'll have to do the whole semester over. That'll make it another whole year before I graduate."

"Are you trying to say that you mean to go back to school as though nothing had happened?" my mother said.

"And just how do you propose—" my father said, and Bo Jo interrupted him.

"It's all set. We are going to live with my folks, and I'll get a job afternoons and weekends. . . ."

"*Your* family?" Mother said, and whipped around to look at me. "Have you consented to this, July?"

"I didn't know what else," I said, and Father said, "Well, now you do."

"Bo Jo," I said, "would you really lose a *whole* semester? I mean, couldn't you take a correspondence course or something?"

"What if he loses a whole year!" my father said. "It's no one's fault but his own."

"If you are going to live with anyone," Mother said, "it should be here with us."

"You promised not to let me down," Bo Jo said to me in a trapped voice. But I was feeling trapped too.

"And I asked you to at least listen," I said. "They're only trying to help us."

"Sure," Bo Jo said, "their way." He had finished his iced tea, but he still held onto the glass. With both hands as though it was something to hang on to.

"I think you should show July *some* consideration," Mother said.

"And I can't believe your family is really happy about your present plan," Father said. "Your father is a foreman, is he not?"

"A construction engineer," Bo Jo said.

"Maybe they will feel differently when they know there is an alternative," Mother said.

"They want me to finish school," Bo Jo said. "They want me to go to college. That's all they want in life."

"But you're young," Mother said. "You've plenty of time."

"First things first," Father said.

Bo Jo put his glass down on the table beside his chair. "July knows how I feel."

"But how do you think *I* feel?" I said, not looking at him. "I don't blame you for not wanting to live with my family. In fact, I understand. Why can't you be understanding too? It isn't just that I don't want to live with your family. I'm scared. I haven't even met them, and they haven't even met me, and how do you know we won't just hate each other? I mean, when we *had* to, well, it was just one of those things but now . . ."

"My head's in knots," Bo Jo said. "I can't think straight anymore." He rubbed his head.

"Why don't you sleep on it?" Mother said. "Why don't you two stay here tonight and sleep on it?"

"Because we're staying at my house," Bo Jo said, and looked at me. "At least, I am."

"Me too, naturally," I said. Actually I would have liked nothing better than to have gone up to my own room and crawled into my own bed, but I couldn't let Mother and Father know it. We all stood up then, but no one moved. Everybody was waiting for the other one to make the break, start for the door. It was very awkward, and for a minute I thought Mother was going to bust out crying, which would have been absolutely gruesome, because I would have blubbered right along with her and this whole mature married image I was trying to give them would have gone up in smoke.

"Remember," Mother said, "tomorrow morning at ten at the chapel. Hadn't you better take along some things? A dress. . . . I thought perhaps the chiffon Aunt Netty sent from Paris. . . ."

"Perfect," I said, and bolted for the stairs.

My room is a corner one and separated from Grace's by a hall and from Gory's by a bathroom and a linen closet, and I've always been very possessive about it. It has a nail on the door where I hang signs: KEEP OUT—PRIVATE PROPERTY, SLEEPING—DO NOT DISTURB, NO TRESPASSING, depending on my mood. The door was open today, and there wasn't any sign on it.

As usual, I had left things in a mess, but unlike usual, Mother had picked up. Everything looked tidy and unused. I even thought she must have washed the paisley spread and dusted down the Degas prints. I got the Paris dress out of the closet. I wanted to take some other things besides clothes, but I didn't know what. I looked around and pretended the house was on fire and I had only minutes to make up my mind. I ended up with the musical powder box with a dancing lady on top, a scrapbook of my favorite poetry, and my new Joan Baez album, though I didn't know whether or not Bo Jo had a record player. I went out of the room still pretending the house was on fire and didn't look back.

Downstairs everybody was hanging around the hall, and just as I got there Grace and Gory, back from Grandmother Greher's, slammed in the front door. I found that for the first time in my life I felt shy with Grace, so I concentrated on Gory, who looked mainly mad, and I said, "Hi, Gory. Meet your new brother. You've always said you wanted one."

Gory looked at Bo Jo as though he weren't there, and Bo Jo looked at me as though he wished he could just melt away into the woodwork, and Grace said, "I think it's very exciting. I hope you'll be very happy, both of you." After that, she didn't seen to know what to say, and neither did I.

It was a stiff and empty moment.

"Let's get going," Bo Jo said. "Ma is looking for us to be there for supper."

Bo Jo lives in a new part of town that sprang up about five years ago when they built a furniture plant out on Otter Road. The houses are all prefab ranch type with picture windows, and any one of them off by itself somewhere would be cute, but they are all pretty much the same shape and much too close together. The house Bo Jo stopped the truck in front of was blue, and the mailbox was in the shape of a stagecoach with the name CARSON JONES spelled out in metal letters on top of it.

We decided to leave my things in the truck so as not to rub it in that we were married until I'd at least met his family. The insides of my hands were cold and sweaty, and my heart was acting the way it does when I have to read a poem I've written aloud to the class in creative writing. Bo Jo didn't look too well either.

The front door was open and television voices and a smell of cooking was coming out of it. Bo Jo walked in, and I followed him. There was a square, stocky, bald-headed man sitting in his shirt sleeves watching television. Bo Jo said, "Hi, Pop," and the man turned and looked at us, or rather he looked at me, and then he got up very slowly and walked over and turned off the television.

"Greetings," he said, without any exclamation point after it, and then he went to the far door and called, "Fanny! They're here." Bo Jo's mother came in wiping her hands on a flouncy apron. She was tall and big, not fat, big, and had eyes like Bo Jo's, only not nearly as blue and clear, blondish hair and a sad mouth wearing orange lipstick.

"So this is July," she said. "Where are your things? I've got the room all ready." I think she was trying to smile at me, but something went wrong and it was more like a grimace.

"They're in the car," I said.

"We thought we'd break the ice first," Bo Jo said.

"Have a seat," Bo Jo's father said, and brushed a cat that I hadn't noticed was there off the sofa.

"Just a minute," Bo Jo's mother said, "I'll have to check the roast."

When she came back, she had taken off the apron and underneath it she had on a blue silk dress with gold sequins across the front, and I wondered if they were going out somewhere after supper.

"Why don't you get your things," she said, "and let me show you your room?"

"I'll get them," Bo Jo said.

His mother and I went down a hall with doors on each side. "This is the master bedroom," Mrs. Jones said as we passed one of them, "and Bo Jo's room," as we passed
58

another. "The house isn't real big," she said, "but after some of the places we've lived, it's good enough for me. Three bedrooms and a kitchen you can really turn around in. With the girls off and gone, it's as much or more than we need. Here we are. . . ." She stood back and waited for me to go in ahead of her. "It may seem small to you coming like you do from the old part of town where all the houses have spread to them, but it gets the morning sun, and it's right next to the bathroom."

It did seem small to me. And pretty awful. There were twin beds with orange taffeta spreads on them and little multicolored shiny silk pillows in bunches at the head. There were twin windows with orange taffeta curtains hanging to the floor, and there was a glass-topped dressing table with an orange taffeta skirt and ribbons of lace around the edges. The walls were a kind of pale green, and on one of them was a picture of a garden with a man and woman swooning on a bench beside a fountain and on another a picture of the Swiss Alps and a chalet in the distance.

"My girls," Mrs. Jones said, "like pretty things. They made these drapes themselves, and I only helped a little with the spread." She was looking at me, waiting for me to say something, but no sound came out for a minute and then I heard myself telling her that it was just darling, which was actually the ghastly truth. Just then Bo Jo came in with the Paris dress and my overnight bag and the dancing lady powder box and the poetry notebook and the Joan Baez album. I could see Mrs. Jones' eyes taking inventory, and it all of a sudden clobbered me that she was Bo Jo's mother and therefore my mother-in-law and that we were related in a very personal way.

"What a beautiful dress, a truly beautiful frock," she said, touching the Paris chiffon with the tips of her fingers. "Where on earth will you wear it now?"

"To the church," Bo Jo said. "We're being married all over again tomorrow morning by a preacher." The way he said it you could tell how *he* felt about it.

"Mother is going to call you," I said. "She wants you to come . . . of course. You and Bo Jo's father."

"But what's the sense of it?" Mrs. Jones said.

59

"They thought it would make things easier," I said, "for everybody."

"Not for me," Mrs. Jones said, "not for us," and she looked at me, really looked at me, for the first time as though she was taking me in. "I am trying to rise above this thing that has happened to us, to our boy. No use crying over spilled milk. But I'll not go to any wedding under such circumstances. It would be a sacrilege." Her eyes filled up with tears, and she turned around and went out of the room.

"And you feel just the way she does," I cried at Bo Jo. "I know you do."

"That may be, but you've got to believe me I wouldn't have let on if I'd known she was going off the deep end like that. Gee, kid," he put his arms around me, awkward and protective, "I'm sorry."

"Thanks," I said. What I meant was thanks for making like a husband, but I didn't think he'd want to hear it.

A bell tinkled at the back of the house, and Bo Jo said, "That means we eat. She always rings a bell. She thinks it gives class."

"I'll put on a new face," I said, "and be right along."

At the door he stopped and turned about. "I can dig where this maybe isn't going to work, living here, I mean. Maybe I'm going to have to wave the white flag and knuckle under and do it your old man's way but don't mention it tonight. Not tonight, hunh?"

"Not for the world," I said.

On my way to the dining room, which actually turned out to be one end of the kitchen, I stopped by Bo Jo's room and looked in. It was not much bigger than a closet and like a closet, it was full of things. An autographed football hung from the light fixture in the ceiling, and the walls were plastered with pennants and cartoons cut from magazines. There was a bed covered with a Navajo blanket and a bureau covered with schoolbooks, a china beer mug with a mermaid painted on it, a bottle of aftershave lotion, and there was an old wicker chair with cushions in it and a beat-up trombone beside it. There wasn't anything except maybe the football that reminded me of Bo Jo, which gave me a very strange feeling, because after all, this was him just the way my room was me. And it made

60

me realize how little we actually knew about each other. How far apart we were. Not just male and female far apart because I adore Gory's room, which is full of collections of bugs and butterflies and books about Egypt and Africa and plane models waiting to be put together, and I would know it belonged to Gory even if it was in Timbuctoo, and I didn't know he lived there. But I wouldn't have known this was Bo Jo's room if I hadn't been told.

They were waiting for me at the mahogany table at the end of the kitchen, and there were lace doilies at the places and long-stemmed glasses and silver spoons, forks, and knives in a heavy flowery pattern which, although I didn't know it then, Mrs. Jones used only on very special occasions Bo Jo got up and pulled back my chair, and as a result his father gave him a look which made him blush and almost knock me over as he shoved the chair under me.

I said, "I didn't know you played the trombone."

"I play Ta Ra Ra Boom De-Ay. That's all I play."

He bought it at a pawnshop with the first money he ever made. Selling papers," Mrs. Jones said. "He used to dream of playing with a band."

"Like your meat rare or well done?" Mr. Jones asked me.

"Rare," I said. The roast looked marvelous with carrots and onions and browned potatoes all around. There was also rice and gravy and sweet potato casserole and fresh green peas and a tossed salad with biscuits.

"Goodness," I said, "I'll never eat all this."

"You've got to at least make a try for it," Mr. Jones said. "She's been in the kitchen all afternoon."

"We don't always eat like this," Mrs. Jones said huffily, and I realized she was trying to tell me that this was for us, special for Bo Jo and me and that probably the blue silk dress with the gold sequins was too. And it was her way of trying to rise above what had happened, like she said.

Nobody talked much at the table. They just ate. They had to, to get through all that food. I tried not to think of our dinner table at home where everyone talks at once. Which is how we keep up with each other's lives.

I offered to help with the dishes, but Mrs. Jones

wouldn't let me, so I went into the living room where Bo Jo and his father were watching a western on television and sat down on the sofa and tried not to go to sleep. I finally gave up and told everybody "Good night," including Bo Jo, who looked as though he didn't quite know what to do about it, and went back to the orange taffeta room and went to bed. I didn't wake up until morning. The other bed hadn't been slept in. I was about to panic when someone knocked and Bo Jo came in. He was wearing a short-at-the-cuffs blue serge suit that looked like church and wasn't nearly as good on him as the madras jacket.

He said, "Up and at 'em, it's almost nine o'clock."

I said, "Where have you been all night?"

He blushed and said, "In my room . . . with Ma and Pop sitting there watching me. I didn't have the nerve . . . like you said, why rub it in?"

I got the picture, and I couldn't blame him. He kissed me to prove to himself there weren't any hard feelings and told me to hurry up or we'd be late to the church. As Mrs. Jones said, the bathroom was right next to my room. It was small and smelled of shaving cream and wet towels and a musty kind of bath powder. There was a clean towel and cloth with the used ones, which I figured must be for me. I wanted to take a bath, but there was a slightly gray ring around the tub from someone else's, so I showered instead. I put on the Paris dress, but the mirror over the dressing table was small and I couldn't see much. I wished there were someone there like my mother or Grace or Mary Ann to tell me that I looked lovely or if my slip showed or whether I needed more lipstick. In fact, for a minute I felt very alone in the world, and then I happened to look at the clock and dashed down the hall and through the living room to the kitchen so I'd have time for a cup of coffee at least. The sink was full of breakfast dishes, and I guessed Mr. Jones was long gone, but Bo Jo and his mother, who was in her bathrobe, were drinking coffee at the table. No lace doilies this morning but a plastic table cover that was supposed to look like maple.

Mrs. Jones looked up from the woman's section of the

62

paper and said, "Pot's on the stove. Would you like some toast?"

Bo Jo looked up from the sports section and said, "Tommy Ryan made all-state track."

I got my coffee and Mrs. Jones said, "Your mother called me on the phone. It was nice of her, considering."

"She's a nice person," I said.

"When I told her we weren't coming to the church," Mrs. Jones said, "she wanted us to come to their house later when Carson gets off work . . . to talk about plans was what she said, but I told her we had our plans made."

"Aw, Ma," Bo Jo said, "why take it out on them? They're just as upset as you and Pop."

"I wasn't taking anything out. I thought our plans were made." She looked upset.

"Well, sure," Bo Jo said, "but that's no reason to snub them cold."

The idea of Mrs. Jones snubbing my parents cold I found hilarious in a sick sort of way.

"I wasn't snubbing anybody. I just wanted it clear where we stand. That we won't be pushed into anything or out of anything."

"Aw, Ma." Bo Jo sighed.

"Why else would they be in such a hurry to meet us? I know what they want. I've got daughters of my own, and I know what I'd want in their shoes. I'd want everything made right for my girl and devil take the boy who'd got her in such a mess. I don't know what their plan is, but I bet my bottom dollar it doesn't have anything to do with you finishing school, going on to college, making your own life."

I had to hand it to her for clairvoyance. Just for something to do I looked at my watch.

"We've got to run," I said.

"Right," Bo Jo said, and pushed back his chair.

At the door he stopped and looked back at his mother, and I thought he wanted to say something or to hear her say something, but she'd already picked up the paper again and a pencil and was starting the crossword puzzle. I was a little behind Bo Jo, and as I went out the front door I heard a sound coming from the kitchen that could have been a sob. It also could have been a chair leg scraping back against the floor.

To get to the chapel where we were to be married for the second time in three days we had to go down Burdine past the high school. First period Monday morning Bo Jo had biology and I had French, and that is where we would be now if we weren't here in Bo Jo's father's Chevy. I didn't look over that way and neither did Bo Jo, and for something to say I said, "You go to the Methodist Church, don't you?"

"When I go," Bo Jo said. "Pop's the one. Every Sunday regular as a clock."

"Doesn't your mother go with him?"

"Sometimes. She shops around for her religion. One year it's this one and the next that one. There's a new one she's all hepped about now. I don't even know the name. Brand-new."

"I sometimes think that's what I'd like to do. Shop around, I mean. The only reason I'm Episcopalian is because my family is; at least I think that's the only reason. I'd like to find out if it is anyway."

"Why?" Bo Jo said.

"Well, because I don't think that's a very good reason, do you? Just because my family belongs. . . ."

"Depends on how deep religion goes with you."

"That's just what I'm saying. I don't think it goes deep enough with me, and I think it should. With everybody. Not church but what you believe in and why."

"You're too deep for me," Bo Jo said. "I have trouble enough sometimes just believing in God."

We got to the chapel and Bo Jo eased the car into a parking space. Mother and Father's car was right in front of us, and in front of their car I saw to my horror Grandmother Greher's Lincoln. It had never occurred to me that she would be here. Even if Father and Mother had asked her, I couldn't imagine her coming, and the sight of her car turned me hot and cold with nerves. Up until then I'd drawn a veil where Grandmother Greher and Bo Jo and I were concerned. I mean in regards to what had happened. She was a person whose opinion of me mattered. Even though I wasn't even sure I loved her. Or even liked her. I always tried to be my best self when I

64

was around her. I always tried to keep my personality tuned down to middle C and my wits tuned up to high C and my manners out in the open where she could see them. She was no ordinary grandmother spilling over with love and human interest. I don't think she cared a hoot that we were her darling Paul's children, "her own flesh and blood," as the saying goes, and would never have bothered with any of us except on Christmas, Thanksgiving, birthdays, and an occasional Sunday if we hadn't beaten a path to her door. We loved Holly Hill, which was the name she gave to the house out on South Road where she lived. It wasn't a hill, and there was no holly for miles around. It was a big house to start with, and Grandfather Greher had kept adding on to it—stairways and hallways and even a turret where you could look out and see all of Clarks County almost, from the salt marshes to the red clay edge of Georgia. And around it there were ten acres of fields and woods to play in and the old carriage house that I had used the summer I thought I'd like to be an actress and have my own stock company. We sometimes spent a whole day out there and saw her only when she went out or came back from a meeting of the Benevolent Society or a game of bridge when she'd wave to us from the piazza. When she *wanted* to see us she sent us an invitation. In the mail. "Dear July, would you like to come Wednesday at four and have tea," or "The blackberries down by the east pasture are ripe. Come tomorrow morning at nine, and we will pick enough for a pie," and later when I'd begun to wear a bra and to talk to her about modern poetry, "Would you like to spend Friday night? We are having Dr. and Mrs. Jones, lately of Japan, for dinner. I think you might find it illuminating." I never knew who "we" was, but it was always "we." Never "I." She probably meant Grandfather Greher, who died long before I was born. Not that she ever mentioned him, but there was no one else in the house to explain it unless she meant Tilda, the cook, and I hardly think so. Not that Grandmother Greher was a snob. To be a snob you have to look down on people, and she doesn't look down or up or even straight ahead at them. She looks through them to something else.

"What are you hanging back for?" Bo Jo said. "After Saturday this should be a cinch."

"Do you really think so?"

"No," he said.

"At least Saturday we weren't pretending something that isn't."

"I know what you mean," he said, and held my hand walking up the cobble path between the gravestones to the chapel. "Maybe," he said, "everybody that gets married in a church, makes promises in a church, is pretending something."

The chapel door was open, and we could see Reverend Michael standing at the chancel rail waiting, and so we hurried up the stone steps and down the aisle. Mother and Father and Grace and Gory and Grandmother Greher were grouped in a kind of semicircle, like bridesmaids, facing Reverend Michael. They all turned to look at us, and I smiled, or thought I did, but maybe it didn't come off because no one smiled back. Not even Gory.

Somebody had put a spray of pink and white azaleas on the altar, and the stained-glass windows over our heads were adazzle with the morning sun shining through them, and the Reverend Michael's voice reciting the "We are gathered here . . ." was deep and warm. By concentrating on these things I almost managed to forget about the justice of the peace in Buxton and Grandmother Greher and Gory, who got the hiccoughs in the middle of the service, a thing he always does when he's deeply upset.

When it was over, Reverend Michael shook our hands and then he shook Mother's hand and Father's, and Bo Jo shook Mother's hand and then Father's, all very solemn as though this were some sort of agreement between them which had nothing to do with me. And then I introduced Bo Jo, or rather Boswell Johnson Jones, to Grandmother Greher, who said in a puzzled voice, "Why, you can't be a day over sixteen yourself!"

"I'm seventeen," Bo Jo said.

After that we drifted out into the sunshine and stood around among the gravestones and wondered what to do next until Mother said brightly, "We've punch and cookies waiting at home."

"I think I'll forego the festivities," Grandmother Greher

66

said. She has a long, thin face like Father's and hooded lids over her eyes like Father, but unlike Father, whose faces changes with every mood, you never know what she is thinking. It is probably a good thing. "But I brought a little something for the bride. It's in my car. If you'll come with me, July . . ."

That was exactly what I dreaded. Being alone with her. She took my arm. She has arthritis and while she doesn't limp or lean on people, she says an arm helps her walk faster and straighter. I thought if I started talking and kept going . . .

I said, "It was sweet of you to come with so little notice. I'm sure this must have been a big surprise to you, but we just didn't dare tell people until the last minute because we knew they'd think we were too young, which maybe we are, but I've always been old for my age in some ways and in olden times people got married at our age and thought nothing of it. . . ."

"As long as they had a plow, a horse, and a spot of land," Grandmother Greher said. "Where's yours?"

"Bo Jo is going to work, if that's what you mean."

"That is not what I mean," she said, and we were at the car. She took out a key and unlocked the glove compartment. "If this marriage chances to survive," she said, "when you are my age, you will have been married sixty-two years. I can't think of anyone on the face of the earth I would want to live with for sixty-two years, including your grandfather, who was the best company I ever knew." She had in her hand a white jeweler's box, and she seemed to be talking to it as much as to me. "He gave these to me on our wedding day." She opened the box and held it out to me. There were four slim gold bracelets linked together by a gold chain with something engraved on each one. I picked them up and looked closely. FAITH, said one, FORGIVENESS, another, HUMOR, the next, and ETERNAL VIGILANCE, the last.

"Those," Grandmother Greher said, "were the qualities he felt one must strive for in a marriage if it is to be successful. I would like you to have them now."

I took them out of the box and fastened them around my wrist. They felt heavy and cumbersome, and I blurted out my thought. . . .

"I'm surprised you didn't give them to Father to give to Mother when they were married."

"Your mother didn't need them," Grandmother Greher said. "She had love."

Suddenly my knees felt weak. I looked into my grandmother's eyes, and they were old and soft and very tired.

"Thank you," I said, and "thank you" again, and kissed her dry, ripply cheek.

"They won't seem nearly so heavy in time," Grandmother Greher said. She patted my shoulder and got in behind the wheel of the Lincoln and stomped down on the gas, roaring the engine as though she were about to set off at seventy miles an hour.

Bo Jo was waiting in the car to drive us to "the festivities," and I showed him the bracelet. I told him about Grandfather giving it to Grandmother on their wedding day. And why.

"Quite a large order," he said.

"Yes," I said. "I think I'll just take one at a time."

"Starting with?"

"Starting with faith."

"In what, for sweet heaven's sake?"

"In the 'and then they all lived happily ever after' bit."

"You're talking about fairy tales, faith in fairy tales," Bo Jo said.

"Yes, fairy tales and magic and whatever it takes."

"You left out witchcraft," Bo Jo said crossly. He obviously didn't follow, and I didn't really want him to.

"That too," I said, and put my head on his shoulder and looked up at him slant-eyed and teasing, the way I used to do long ago before I had anything to be sorry for or worried about.

"Hey," he said, and grinned a slow grin that started with his eyes, those blue, living-color eyes, and moved down to his mouth, smoothing his face along the way. "Hey," he said again real slow and turned the car into the curb and stopped and right there in broad daylight kissed me. Hard and sweet, the way he used to kiss me long ago before he had anything to be sorry for or worried about.

The "festivities" were a bit of a flop with just my family and the Reverend Michael, and I began to think it really mean of Bo Jo's family to make such a point of not being

68

there. They so obviously weren't there it was as though they were. And hurt.

As soon as the Reverend left, Father and Mother herded us into the study to settle our future. I knew Bo Jo had had a double take about living with his folks, and frankly I felt as though one more night with the orange taffeta and I'd be ready for the loony bin, but I was beginning to feel dimly too that maybe we ought to have a little more time to make up our minds and that it should be our minds that got made up and not everyone else's, but before I could say it, Father had said to Bo Jo, "I talked to our manager, Mr. Fargo, this morning, and he can use you on the IBM machine. You'll be paid while you learn, fifty dollars a week, and he can start you tomorrow morning."

And Mother had said to me, "Hatty Barnes' garage apartment is vacant, forty-five a month, and really quite sweet, though when summer comes, you'll need an air conditioner."

They were looking from one to the other of us like twin Santa Clauses, and Bo Jo looked at me and shrugged. "What's the use?" he said. "What's the ever living use in fighting it? It's what you want, isn't it?"

And, of course, it was. Exactly. I grinned all over myself. I couldn't help it. The relief was too much. And that was that. We moved into the apartment over Hatty Barnes' garage two weeks later.

"Two weeks later," I say, as thought it were no time at all. As though nothing happened in those two weeks. Actually they were action packed.

Mrs. Jones, in a panic for fear her son would never again see another square meal or wear another correctly ironed shirt, tried to give me a crash course in domestic science. I did learn how to cook a roast and make a soup with what was left of it, but I flunked the pastry course completely, and when it came to the ironing I not only burned a hole in one of Bo Jo's shirts but caught the ironing board cover on fire and came close to burning down the house. When it was all over, Mrs. Jones burst into tears and dashed off to her room without a word. She wasn't the sort of person to cry over a hole or a burned-up ironing board cover, and I'm sure that wasn't what she was crying about. I'm sure she was crying over everything

69

that had happened lately, and I didn't blame her. I felt like throwing a slight screaming fit myself.

After a while she came to the door of Bo Jo's sisters' room, where I'd gone to get out of the way and recuperate, and knocked. I was afraid she'd come to explain or worse, to apologize, and I wished I'd gone out for a long walk while the going was good. There's nothing more embarrassing than being apologized to by a grown-up. What on earth do you *say*?

She came in and stood at the end of the orange taffeta bed. Her eyes were still red from crying and all the "tease" was mashed out of her hair so it just looked tired. I offered her the only chair in the room, but she shook her head. She had something to say and she was bursting to say it, and from the look of her I did not think it was going to be an explanation nor an apology.

"When I was your age," she began in a stern voice, staring me down, "I had been cooking three meals a day for years, scrubbing floors, washing, ironing. My father was a good man, but all his life he thought he'd find success in the next town, the next job. One year we moved seven times. My mother was a telephone operator. No matter where we went she could always find work. The only days she missed were moving days, days between towns. My job was to keep the house going. Since I was ten years old I've been keeping some house going. Bo Jo is used to good nourishing food and a clean shirt every morning." She paused and her eyes narrowed. "What can you do for him? What can you do for my son? You don't even know how to make a bed!"

"I made this one," I snapped.

To my horror she jerked back the bedspread. Of course it was a mess. All I'd done was pull up the covers. Without a word she snatched off the blanket, the two sheets. "Here, take this end." She handed me one side of the sheet, and she took the other. "Now top-side first. This is the way the corners go. Fold, and fold, and under . . ."

The announcement of our marriage appeared in the Trilby *Times*.

Mr. and Mrs. John Gregory Greher announce the

marriage of their daughter, July Elizabeth, to Mr. Boswell Johnson Jones on March twelfth in the Chapel of the Redeemer. . . . The ceremony was conducted by the Reverend Stewart Michael.

After a brief honeymoon the couple will make their home at 18 Southwick Way.

Even Bo Jo got a smile out of the honeymoon bit. He hadn't yet moved into his sisters' room with me. And though it was pretty lonesome in there and downright scary a couple of times when I'd wake up in the night and not know where I was, I couldn't blame him. On those nights when we went to bed at the same time his mother always found some reason to follow us down the hall—clean towels for the bathroom, an alarm clock for Bo Jo—and hang around until I went into my room and Bo Jo into his. And when we didn't go to bed at the same time it would have been even more pointed if Bo Jo had tried to sleep in my room because his parents' room was right next door to it and they left their door open all night. I wondered if they always had or if this was their idea of how to chaperone us around the clock, but I didn't ask Bo Jo. He was already embarrassed enough about the situation.

The announcement in the paper didn't create much furor since by that time the news had pretty much gone the rounds. Mother said she got a few hard-to-handle phone calls from so-called friends, but that for the most part people were being very tactful and kind. Mrs. Ryan, Tommy's mother, wanted to have a luncheon or a tea for me, but neither my mother nor I felt up to carrying it off. Mrs. Ryan was very understanding. Mary Ann, however, wasn't. She had been shocked and amazed when she first learned we were married. She called me right up to ask if it were true.

"I just couldn't believe it," she said. "I still can't." And hung up. She called back in a minute, of course, when she'd got herself together and said she wanted to *do* something for me and what would I like? A shower? An evening party, mixed? It was just like her. In that few minutes between calls she had managed to digest the indigestible and was now, without even a hiccup, prepared to do the right and conventional thing.

"I appreciate the thought," I told her, "but I don't think showers are in order *after* you're married and an evening party would just be too much of a thing." I meant for Bo Jo and me.

"I didn't mean anything swoosh. Mother Dina would do all the planning. She's good at it." Mary Ann referred to any current stepmother as Mother whatever her first name was, which sometimes gave those who weren't in the know the idea that she lived in a convent.

"I appreciate the thought," I repeated. "I honestly do, but right now everything is so indefinite . . ." My voice trailed off as I ran out of excuses.

"You sound as though you couldn't care less."

"It isn't that at all."

"What is it then?"

Was it possible that she didn't know? Hadn't guessed? Ever since the announcement in the paper I'd found it hard to go downtown, to meet people on the street. I assumed everyone would know. But Mary Ann wasn't everyone, I reminded myself. The same reasons why I couldn't talk to her in the beginning were the reasons why I couldn't be honest with her now.

"Maybe later," I said, "when we get settled."

"Yes. Sure," she said in a small hurt voice.

Grace came home from school one day when I'd dropped in at the house to pick up some more clothes. . . . I "dropped in" as often as my pride would allow in those days of loneliness and boredom. . . . She was in a rage at the "insinuations" her friends were making about me. Mother gave me a look which told me what to do even if I hadn't already known. I let her keep her rage. And her innocence.

The second evening Bo Jo came home from his new job at the bank his father was sitting in the living room looking at the news. The evening before, Bo Jo had got home before him and was out of his business suit and into slacks and a T shirt by the time Mr. Jones saw him, but this night when Mr. Jones looked up and saw Bo Jo in the new business suit he'd had to charge at Plenty's Depart-

72

ment Store, he half got up out of his chair. "That's a mighty fancy rig you've got on for five o'clock in the afternoon. Where've you been?"

"To the bank," Bo Jo said, and tried to cut through to his room, but Mr. Jones wouldn't let him go.

"So that's to be the uniform," he said, looking Bo Jo up and down as though he were some sort of freak. I honestly don't think he had realized that Bo Jo was starting work so soon.

"Yeah," Bo Jo kind of grinned, "it feels funny going out in the morning all straitjacketed up, but I'll get used to it."

"Sure, you'll get used to it. Sure!" Mr. Jones got all the way out of his chair and stomped out to the kitchen. When he came back, Bo Jo had gone to change his clothes, but I was still sitting there. Mr. Jones had a shot glass of whiskey in one hand and a glass of water in the other. He poured the whisky down and the water after as though it were some kind of medicine he had to take and then he went to the phone.

The phone was in the hallway between the living room—the parlor Mrs. Jones called it—and the kitchen and even in a normal tone of voice anyone in the parlor couldn't help but hear everything that was said. But Mr. Jones wasn't talking in a normal tone of voice. He was talking loud, and it didn't take me long to realize he was talking to my father. "You and your lady wife are ruining my son's life. Ruining him. He's not going to be worth the skin he was born in by the time you get through with him. Why couldn't you leave him alone? Hunh? Why?

"He oughta be in a football helmet and padded pants caked up in mud when he comes in in the afternoon. Not looking like somebody's little vice-president in charge of nothing!"

At this point Mrs. Jones, hearing the shouting, came charging out from the kitchen and grabbed his arm and tried to pull him away from the telephone, but he shook her loose like she was a bug lighting on his sleeve.

"God damn it, what do you and your lady wife know about what a man wants for his boy! What the hell do you know about a man like me or a boy like Bo Jo? What I've worked all my life to do for him—" He broke off and

73

slammed the receiver back on its hook. I sat there too stunned to move, hoping he had forgotten I was there and wouldn't remember now.

"You shouldn't have done it, Carson. There's enough trouble between the families without making more."

"Trouble! What do I care about *more* trouble! More can't hurt us!"

"Don't say that. It might bring us bad luck. Don't say it!" Mrs. Jones said, and began to cry. I was afraid they'd come into the parlor next so I got up and shot down the hall to Bo Jo's room. The door was shut, but I didn't knock, just flung through the door and slammed it shut behind me.

Bo Jo had taken off the business suit, but he hadn't put on his other clothes. He was just wearing his shorts. He was sprawled in or rather across the one big chair and there was a book open in his lap. I had never before seen Bo Jo reading anything purely for pleasure except the newspaper and certain magazines, and I was naturally curious to see what it was. It was last year's high school annual, and it was turned to the page with his picture on it. Alicia Helms' picture was on the same page. He could have been looking at either one. All this I noticed with just half my mind. Actually I was still churning away with what had happened in the other room.

"I just can't stay here any longer," I told Bo Jo. "The way your father talked to mine! As though he were some sort of, sort of . . . It was unfair! My father has only tried to help us. So your life is ruined! What about mine?"

Bo Jo closed the annual and put it down on the floor beside his chair and after glancing toward the door to make sure it was shut pulled me down so I was sitting crosswise beside him in the chair with one of his arms hooked around me.

"Start at the beginning," he said, "only this time set the speed at thirty-three."

So I told him from the beginning, and when I finished, Bo Jo said, "I'm sorry, but he didn't really mean anything. That's just the way he is, that's all. And besides, where can we go except to your folks, and that would be just as bad for me as here is for you."

74

"Maybe I could go there and you stay ... just until Hatty Barnes' garage is ready . only a week or so."

"If it's only a week, can't you stick it out here until then and not start a war?"

"He's the one starting the war!"

"It's only a couple of days now. And if you go to your folks and I stay with mine the kids will think we've already busted up."

That I could see and that really bothered me even while I inwardly cringed because I could remember a time when I used to think that people shouldn't care what unimportant and extraneous people thought about them. At least that they shouldn't let that influence what they did. That's what I used to think. Less than two months ago.

"If only you would sleep in your sisters' room," I said, "it would make it easier. I ... I ... feel so out of place in there."

"And you sleep in here?"

"Of course not, stupid!"

"I'll make a try for it," he said, "but you know how it is."

"Yes, I know," I said.

The next day Mrs. Jones called up my mother to apologize for her husband's telephone call to my father and ended by telling her that she and Father were ruining her son's life. At least, according to Mother. That was one telephone conversation I didn't hear I'm happy to say, though Mother didn't seem to be in the least bit upset about it, and two days later took the bull by the horns and came to call on Mrs. Jones. I got the nervous prickles when I saw Mother's station wagon nosing down the street looking for the house.

I was torn between running out to the street to show her where I was and going back to the kitchen to warn Bo Jo's mother, who, I was beginning to know, did not like unexpected callers and would be most especially embarrassed to have my mother find her in an apron and without lipstick on. As I wavered, Mother stopped the car in front of the Jones' and Mrs. Jones came out of the kitchen and peering through the window said, "Who in heaven's name is that?"

"My mother," I said, and couldn't keep the pride out of

my voice. She looked so young and pretty as she alighted from the car and came up the walk. It was a coldish day for March, and she was wearing the heather tweed suit she'd got the wool for in Scotland and a small imp of a hat on the back of her head and flat heels so that she didn't look as tall as usual.

I expected Mrs. Jones would fly to her bedroom untying the apron as she went, but she surprised me. Without even a glance at the parlor mirror or a pat to her hair, she went to the door and opened it and stood waiting for my mother to come through it.

"Pleased to meet you, I'm sure," she said to my mother, lifting her chin slightly and standing back to let my mother pass her. But neither of them offered the other a hand.

What I wanted to do was rush right up and give my mother a great big hug because I knew what she was doing wasn't easy for her and that Bo Jo's mother wasn't going to make it any easier. In fact, for a minute I was afraid she wasn't even going to invite my mother to sit down, that the two of them would just stand there looking each other over and trying to pretend that that was not what they were doing at all.

"I thought it time I met July's mother-in-law," my mother said with a kind of wry smile that turned me inside out.

"I suppose it is inevitable," Bo Jo's mother said. "Won't you be seated?" And as my mother started to sit in the nearest chair she added, "I think you'll find this one more comfortable. . . ." But as my mother let herself down in the flowered armchair Bo Jo's mother indicated, Mrs. Jones shook her head, "No, no, this blue one here would be better, I think. The springs are newer."

It was like a game of musical chairs with only one person, my mother, playing. If I hadn't known that the big thing Bo Jo's mother lacks is a sense of humor I would have thought she was doing the chair bit on purpose to make my mother look ridiculous, but obviously there was nothing ridiculous in this performance to Mrs. Jones. However, I noticed the corners of Mother's mouth begin to twitch, and I was afraid if our eyes met we'd break up

76

so I didn't look at her again until she was squared away in the blue chair with the newer springs.

"Can I fix you some coffee?" Mrs. Jones said.

"That would be very nice," my mother said.

"Cream and sugar?"

"Please."

"Canned milk is what we use for cream. That all right with you?"

"Splendid," my mother lied.

"Really, July," my mother whispered as soon as she'd left the room, *"you* should have offered to help her."

"She wouldn't have let me," I whispered back. "She doesn't trust me with her good china." I somehow thought that for this occasion Bo Jo's mother would bring out the "good" china. But she didn't. I guess she felt the business about being sure Mother got the best chair was about as much in the airs and graces department as she could manage in one day. Anything more than that would have been "putting on," which in her books was as deadly a sin as a straight-out lie. That's one thing I have to hand the woman. She was just as tough on herself as she was on everyone else.

"Sorry about our talk yesterday." Mrs. Jones set down a tray with the pot the coffee had been made in on it and the blue pottery cups we used for breakfast every morning and a plate of cheese pastries she'd made just the day before. "Glad you didn't let it stand between our getting acquainted."

"Of course not," my mother exclaimed. "At a time like this all tempers are short and tongues too quick. I never gave it another thought." And I caught myself thinking that if Bo Jo's mother would believe that, she would believe anything.

"Well, *I* did," Bo Jo's mother said, and gulped her coffee down the same way Mr. Jones had gulped down his whiskey just before going to the phone to call my father the other night.

"Well, you shouldn't have," my mother said, and I wondered what I could possibly say to get them out of this groove and going on something else.

It was then I first realized that the sort of thing I would pick to say to my mother was not the sort of thing that would interest Mrs. Jones nor was the sort of conversation I carried on with Mrs. Jones when Bo Jo wasn't there likely to intrigue my mother. In fact, she would probably think I had lost my mind. Because when I was alone with Mrs. Jones I tried to act like Bo Jo's wife and very mature for my age.

"July tells me you have two other children," Mrs. Jones said. It must have been Bo Jo who told her. I never told her anything because she never asked me. Bo Jo could have found me under a cabbage leaf for all she seemed to know or care.

"Yes, Grace is fourteen, Gory twelve," my mother said, as though that covered it, which as far as she was concerned, it did. She was never one to talk about her children, any more than she would talk about herself.

"I have two daughters," Mrs. Jones said, beginning to look more like herself. "Fine girls, both of them. Would you like to see their pictures?"

She was back in no time with the leather folding frame she kept on her bureau and had shown me the second day I was there. "This is Alice in her nurse's uniform . . . she's at Grady in Atlanta. Pediatrics. Some day she hopes to get a degree in it. . . . I don't know just how it works, but if she says she's going to do something, she will. And this is Betty Sue . . . her real name is Elizabeth Susan. I try to give my children good strong names but something always happens to twist them around . . . except for Alice . . . Betty Sue is married. Her husband travels. For a plastic company. Betty Sue still works. She always did want nice things and figures to have them. Of course, I'd like a grandchild, but that's up to her to decide—" She broke off and looked at my mother and suddenly, like Bo Jo when he's mad or upset, her ears began to turn red, only with her it went all over her face and down her neck. I knew what had happened. She had remembered that she *was* going to have a grandchild. If she could bring herself to call it that. Or think of it even.

"July," my mother said, "would you go out to the car and bring me my cigarettes?"

I have said my mother seldom smokes, but I didn't blame her for wanting to now. However, there were no cigarettes in the car, not on the seat, not in the glove

78

compartment, nor did she usually carry any with her, I remembered finally. I got the message. I stayed out in the car for about fifteen minutes. The keys were in the ignition where Father is always scolding her for leaving them so I turned on the radio and listened to a quiz program in which you could win a washing machine if you wrote in the correct answers to their questions. The apartment over Hatty Barnes' garage didn't have a washing machine. I listened very carefully and wrote down the questions and the address of the station that broadcast the program on the back of Mother's marketing list with a pencil I found in the seat crack.

When I went back inside, Mother and Mrs. Jones were both dabbing at their eyes. In a friendly sort of way. And when Mother left, Mrs. Jones gave her her recipe for the cheese pastries because Mother had admired them so much. I knew how much her personal recipes meant to Mrs. Jones. I also knew that Mother would have forgotten all about it before she got home and wouldn't remember it again until she cleaned out her pocketbook when she would toss it into the wastebasket along with all the accumulation of trading stamps, shopping lists, and golf scores. It made me feel sorry for Bo Jo's mother, though I don't know why it should have. She'd never find out.

Gory broke into his piggy bank and bought me a cookbook for a wedding present. I was terribly pleased, especially since he had avoided me ever since that gruesome Sunday just after we were married when I'd tried to sell him Bo Jo as a new brother.

Bo Jo had a talk with the principal at Trilby High, hoping that there still might be some way he could work toward a diploma on the side, but it was no use. There was no way Bo Jo could finish out his credits for the semester without attending classes.

Mother fainted in the supermarket, But Dr. Hapgood said it was just nerves.

Grandmother Greher invited Bo Jo and me for supper. Like most of her invitations, it arrived by mail:

DEAR JULY:

Unless I hear to the contrary we shall expect you and your young man for dinner Thursday evening at seven. Perhaps he (you will forgive me if I cannot at the moment recall his name) would like to view the African safari slides afterwards. Or would he prefer cards? We can decide that later.

It was signed Louisa Conduit Greher as were all her notes or letters to me from that day onward. I don't know whether she simply forgot to call herself Grandmother or didn't want to be a grandmother to anyone old enough, however young that might be, to have got themselves married.

Bo Jo began by flatly refusing to go. He said he was having a hard enough time getting used to my parents without tackling *"that* old lady."

I said, "What's so wrong with her?"

"It's not what's wrong with *her,*" Bo Jo said, "it's what's wrong with me. I feel everything that's wrong with me sticking out all over me the minute she looks at me."

I knew what he meant as I'd felt much the same myself, so I didn't argue the point. I said, "However, she makes you feel she likes you. If she didn't, she wouldn't ask us."

"She has to do it," Bo Jo said. "Family solidarity. Chin up. Show the world. . . . You are still her granddaughter whatever you may have married."

"You are wrong about her. She never does anything she doesn't want to do."

"Besides, there's a hell of a good baseball game on TV that night."

"I really think this is something we ought to do whether we want to or not."

"Why? What's she to you besides being an old lady that happens to be your grandmother?"

I had to think about that. "She's someone I respect," I said after a moment. "I think I probably respect her more than anyone I know. But don't ask me why. She's never *done* anything but just *be.* Maybe that *is* why."

"You're too deep for me," Bo Jo said, "and O.K., you win, BUT the African safari bit is out. Understand?"

80

I hadn't been out to Holly Hill since Christmas and, as always, when I hadn't been there for a while everything looked smaller and shabbier than I remembered it. I don't know what Bo Jo had expected, but he seemed relieved when he first saw the house. It is a plain up and down sort of house with wide porches running around three sides of the lower floor. Because it was built over a hundred years ago the kitchen is separated from the main house by a roofed runway leading off the downstairs hall so that if the kitchen should catch fire, which is where most fires started in those days, the rest of the house needn't burn down too.

"The way you talked about the place," Bo Jo said, "I thought it was going to be some sort of an old Southern mansion."

"But I didn't talk about it," I said, "not the house, only about the carriage house ... over there," I pointed to the left of the road, "and the pine wood and the blackberry bushes alongside the railroad track beyond the east pasture." I pointed off to the right. "I never even mentioned the house that I can remember."

Bo Jo thought this over for a minute and said, "I guess it wasn't anything you said gave me the idea. I guess it's the way the old lady looks. White columns two stories high and old empty slave quarters out back is how she looks."

"You're thinking Hollywood," I said. "Most of the old houses around here were built as summer houses to get away from the mosquitoes and the heat on the plantations inland. The slaves stayed back on the plantation to keep it going. Not that my grandmother would know. She's a Yankee from Vermont. Married my grandfather when he went north to Harvard. One of the first things she did after he died was to take down all the portraits of the Greher ancestors. 'I never knew those people,' she said, 'and from the look of most of them I wouldn't care to.' "

"That's a load off my mind," Bo Jo said. "I had the idea she was some sort of a snob."

I didn't say anything because actually, I suppose, she was. About certain things like good manners and honesty and keeping an open mind about things. When she liked a person, she always said they kept an open mind and when

81

she didn't like someone, the worst she could find to say about them was that they had a closed mind. "I am not interested in opinions," she'd often say. "Opinions are the children of a closed mind. It's ideas that make life interesting and exciting."

I knew she'd find Bo Jo honest and his manners O.K. However, I frankly didn't know how he'd measure up on the open mind part. I simply didn't know yet whether Bo Jo's mind was open or closed. Or whether he had "opinions" or "ideas" or either one. As we parked in front of the house and Bo Jo got out I decided not to care. I decided if Grandmother Greher was going to like Bo Jo it had already been settled and if she wasn't going to like him that had been settled too. He was, after all, my husband, for better or worse, and she could take it or leave it.

"Goodness, child," she said to me first thing, "I'd not realized what a stubborn little chin you have when you poke it out a bit," and to Bo Jo, "I am going to have a small glass of champagne. I always have one before dinner. Would you like to join me?"

Bo Jo gave me a questioning look as if to say should he or shouldn't he. He didn't like champagne. He said it gave him a headache. I think it also reminded him of the night the school punch got spiked and that that is really what gave him the headache, whether he knew it or not.

I didn't give him any answer and in a minute he said, "Thanks a lot, Mrs. Greher, but I'd rather have a Coke if you've got it . . . or maybe a beer."

"Splendid," Grandmother Greher said, and with the pewter bell that she carried around with her from room to room she rang for Mathilda. "And you, of course," she said to me, "will have ginger ale as usual."

Dinner went fairly smoothly though I'd forgotten to brief Bo Jo in on what forks for what and he had to wait and see which one I picked up for this and that. I don't think Grandmother Greher noticed. She was much too busy "drawing him out." I learned more about him in that one evening than I'd ever known before. I didn't know, for instance, that he'd been born in Panama or that he had an uncle in Texas whom he'd never met but when he was nine he "borrowed" a bicycle and set out for Texas to meet him because he lived on a ranch and was, according to Bo Jo's father, loaded. He had planned to get his uncle to ship the bicycle back as soon as he got there but, of course, no one believed *that* and he'd had to pay the boy from whom he'd "borrowed" it twenty-five dollars—all the money he'd saved in his entire life ... though he'd got no further than the next town—and was forced to go to church with his mother every Sunday for a year.

I didn't know that when he was little he had wanted to be a civil engineer because he liked to build dams. One time they lived in the mountains and any brook or stream he'd come to he had stopped and built a dam across it. He liked to watch the water rise upstream because of the dam he'd built. He also liked to make a hole in the dam when it was all finished and channel the water any way he wanted it to go. I got a picture then for a minute: a little boy with bristly hair and eyes that shone with accomplishment and power as he watched a stream going the way he had made it go.

"You never tell *me* anything," I said later.

"You never ask," he said.

Grandmother Greher hadn't asked either. She had a way of getting people to talk about themselves without realizing they were doing it.

After dinner to my amazement I heard Bo Jo *asking* to see the African slides. We set up the projector in what was once Grandfather's study and still held his old pipe racks and his collection of first editions. Grandmother showed Bo Jo how to use it. I'd seen the slides a dozen times or more but they still delighted me. They delighted Bo Jo too. It was Grandmother Greher who went to sleep in the straight-backed chair.

She must have some built-in alarm system because as the last slide was clicked into place her eyes flashed open and she straightened her shoulders.

"Most amusing," she said, "most amusing. Particularly the one of our guide being chased by the monkey."

She helped put the slides away and saw us to the door and out onto the piazza where the moonlight spread down the steps and across the fields to the woods' edge. Acres and acres of moonlight and far away a mourning dove was crying.

"Such a beautiful night for young lovers." She looked at us and sighed. "Such a beautiful night. . ." She smiled then and blew us a kiss and we walked down the steps hand in hand.

And that night Bo Jo slept in the orange taffeta room with the door closed and bolted behind us. The only concession we made to his mother was to make the twin bed that had not been slept in look as though it had.

One night Mary Ann came by with Rodney and Charlie and Gail and we went to the drive-in and afterwards to the Coffee Pot and made like old times. With a difference. The group used always to go dutch at the Pot. When it came up my turn to feed the noise box Bo Jo paid my fare. Likewise the quarter bet I made and lost to Rodney on who wrote the lyrics for *Mame*. And of course the final Coke and hamburger bill. It made me feel that while he was still a part of the group, I somehow wasn't. And then they began talking about school and we were both "out." We tried to join in but there were too many little details we didn't know and by the time they'd stop to clue us in, the story would have lost its punch. Even the way we kidded each other had changed. Or rather the way we didn't. There were too many subjects that were not funny anymore. Too many touchy areas. I realized that in the space of a few days we had put so much distance between us that even if they ran like mad and we stood perfectly still, we'd never be all together, in the same place, again. It was a somewhat sad and lonely feeling and after they'd dropped us off at Bo Jo's house, I stayed out on the front stoop and looked at the moon. The same moon that Grandmother Greher had admired a few nights earlier. It was smaller now and lopsided. Bo Jo went inside where his father was watching the Late Show and watched it with him until it was over.

When it was over, he came outside and said, "Aren't you ever going to bed?"

Once we were in bed I asked him if he didn't feel sort of scared about how fast things were changing between us and all our friends.

"Not scared," he said. "I just notice a difference but everybody's bound to feel a little funny at first. Wait until we get into our own place. They'll be swarming like bees. We'll be the only high school kids in town with a place of our own. It'll be a regular hangout." He sounded pleased. I wasn't so sure that I was. I hadn't exactly thought of a place of our own as a hangout. I'd thought more in terms of getting to know each other better and having a little privacy.

We moved into our apartment on a Sunday. Bo Jo's father lent us the truck, but we didn't need it. There wasn't that much to move. All that we took from Bo Jo's were his clothes, the autographed football, the trombone, and the things I'd already moved over there. From my house we took all of my books that the one bookcase in the apartment would hold, my radio and stereo hi-fi, and a few of my clothes. I would come back and pick up more later. Frankly I was embarrassed to have Bo Jo see how many clothes I had.

Hatty Barnes' garage was bigger than most, so the apartment was bigger than most garage apartments and she hadn't tried to cram a lot of rooms into the space. There were only two and a bath. The living room and kitchen and dining room were one room in the shape of an L, and the bedroom opened off the long end, which was the living room.

It really was terribly cute and even though the furniture was obviously left over from a rummage sale, it was clean and comfortable and Miss Hatty Barnes gave us permission to scrape it or paint it or anything short of burn it. Actually I wouldn't have cared if we'd been moving into the garage itself with no furniture, I was so glad to be out of that orange taffeta bedroom.

We had planned to spend the whole day moving, but it didn't take us any time at all to hang up our clothes and put the books in the bookcase. By eleven A.M. we were done and the big question was Now What? I mean, here we were with everything in place and the whole long day to do just what we pleased, and what was there to do? We just looked at each other waiting for the other one to take over. It was too late for church and too early for the movies and not nearly time for lunch since we'd had a huge breakfast before we left Bo Jo's house a few hours earlier. We didn't have a car and we didn't have television

85

and we didn't have homework anymore. All these things went through my mind in a kind of panic, and I went over and put a record on the stereo. The one on top of the pile. It turned out to be a Bobby Darin.

"I think," Bo Jo said, "I'll mosey on down to the Coffee Pot." Just like that he said it! No if you please or would I like to come along.

"Have fun," I said coldly.

"Well, what else?" he said. "I mean if there's anything you want me to do around here"—he looked around here at everything in its place—"but I thought everything was . . ."

"It is," I said. "Worry not. As I said before, have fun!"

"You don't sound as though you mean it," he said. "In fact," he said, "you sound as though you resent the idea."

"Why on earth should I?" I said.

"Don't ask me. What I know about girls you could put on the point of a pin—"

"Then put it there," I said, and stomped into the bedroom and shut the door and sat down on the bed and waited for him to say he was sorry. I'd forgotten to put the arm down on the record player so it would turn off by itself. When the Bobby Darin had played through three times, I cracked the door and looked out, but there wasn't anybody there. He'd already gone. I took off the Bobby Darin and put on a Rachmaninoff concerto and went and looked out the door. The door looked out on Hatty Barnes' driveway and down the street. Bo Jo was still in sight so he must have given the pros and cons a little thought before he took off.

I went and looked in the icebox. Mother had stocked it the day before with enough food to feed an army for a week, but I wasn't hungry. I got out a Coke and went and sat on the sofa and listened to the concerto. There was a window right behind the sofa that looked down on Hatty Barnes' rose garden and terrace. The terrace had white wrought-iron chairs and a table, and pretty soon Hatty and a woman under a big hat came out carrying iced-tea glasses.

Across from the sofa the wall around the bookcase looked bare, and I decided what it needed were my prints from home. The voices of Hatty Barnes and the lady in the pink hat floated up through the open window, but I couldn't hear what they were saying because of the Rachmaninoff so I turned it off.

Even with the stereo off the acoustics weren't too good. I could hear Hatty Barnes. She has a slightly high-pitched voice with a kind of rollicking lilt to it that carries, but Pink Hat's voice was softer and only when her head was half turned my way could I hear what she said, which made for some interesting effects.

HATTY BARNES: I dare say you are right about Lillian. She isn't actually chairman material. Perhaps we should put her on the altar guild.

PINK HAT: . . . . . in memory of Horace.

HATTY BARNES: How brave of Cara to declare herself. Or perhaps just possessive. Perhaps she wanted the whole town to know that he had belonged to her.

PINK HAT: Or she to him . . . . . your garage?

HATTY BARNES: The dearest little couple. High School babies really. I feel awfully sorry for the parents—She's Paul and Agnes Greher's daughter—I know they must be half out of their minds. But I shall find it most entertaining. Much more so than that schoolteacher with the braids around her head who folk danced.

Pink Hat's back was to me. I could hear the faint hum of her voice but no words. The voice when I did hear it was familiar, but I couldn't place it nor could I get a good look at her face under that huge hat.

PINK HAT, turning her head a little: . . . . . absolutely silly of you not to.

HATTY BARNES: No, I mustn't. I get much too attached.

PINK HAT: Better to have loved and lost.

HATTY BARNES: No one knows that better than I.

PINK HAT: . . . . . became of Mr. Bones?

HATTY BARNES: He left me for the prize cat of the year. I got tired of hauling him home by the scruff of his neck. Too humiliating. So finally I just stopped going to look for him. I suppose he's still there. I do know toward the last the owners of the Angora had begun to feed him too.

I wished they would go back to talking about Bo Jo and me, but they didn't and so pretty soon I turned the Rachmaninoff back on again and pretty soon I went to sleep. It was one o'clock when I woke up, and Bo Jo was there asking about lunch just as though nothing had happened.

I've never cooked much except eggs and hamburgers and chocolate fudge. Among other things Mother had given us a baked ham. I rustled up a pineapple and cottage cheese salad and some brown-and-serve rolls to go with it, and that was lunch. Afterwards Bo Jo sat cross-legged on the floor and practiced trills on his trombone. It was almost time for the movies so I changed my dress and put on a clean face.

When I came out of the bedroom, Bo Jo said, "Where are you going?"

I said, "To the movies, natch."

He said, "It's a lousy show, all about a girl who's deaf, dumb, and blind."

"I know all about it," I said. "I've wanted to see it for ages. Besides, we always go to the show on Sunday. . . ."

"That was in the dark ages," he said, and played a few low notes on the trombone. "B.C. Meaning Before Crisis. We now have to think about how we spend our money. Or don't spend it mainly."

"You just don't want to see this show," I said. "You're just making excuses to keep from going."

"That's not so," he said, his ears getting red. "I've sat through plenty worse shows than this with you and not complained. Just where do you think the money's going to come from to have this baby? How do you think we're going to pay the doctor? The hospital?"

The truth was I hadn't given it a thought.

"Just how much did *you* spend at the Coffee Pot this morning?"

"Ten cents," he said, and put down his trombone and stood up. "Ten cents for one lousy cup of coffee."

"You were gone longer than one cup of coffee," I said.

"I ran into some of the team. We got to talking. Any objections?"

"Yes," I said, "it so happens I have. Why couldn't you take me with you?"

"You didn't ask me to."

"How could I? You said you were going. Period. Obviously you didn't want me to come."

"Oh, for Christ's sweet sake!" Bo Jo held his hands

88

against the side of his head as though he were trying to hold it together. "What started all this? What were we talking about? Where were we? The show! You wanted to go to the show! O.K., go to the show!" He dug his hand into his pocket and came out with a dollar bill and slapped it into my hand.

I threw the dollar bill at him and dashed into the bathroom and got sick in the basin. Bo Jo came and held my head and handed me a washcloth to wash my face afterwards.

"It was probably because I ate too fast . . ." I said.

"Or the baby . . ." Bo Jo said.

"It's not a baby yet," I said. "It's an embryo."

"Feel better?"

"Much."

"Better enough so we go to the show?"

"I do," I said, "but it isn't absolutely necessary. I mean you do have a point about the money."

"Just so you see it," Bo Jo said.

I came out of the theatre in a daze. I always find it hard to return to reality after seeing a truly superior performance.

Bo Jo said, "I'm glad you made me see it."

"Unhunh," I said.

"I mean it leaves you with a feeling that nothing is really impossible . . . entirely out of the question . . . unattainable. . . ."

"I know," I said.

"It also leaves you with a new and great respect for communication between people. I mean what would the world, civilization, be like without it?"

"A shambles," I said.

"But you're not really listening," Bo Jo said. "Your mind is somewhere else."

"I was thinking about the summer we put on plays in Grandmother Greher's carriage house. I was thinking about how I used to want to be an actress."

"No more?" Bo Jo grinned, as though natch and of course "no more," and I said:

"Not an actress. A playwright. Some day I want to write a play."

"What about?" Bo Jo said.

"Heavens, how should I know?" I said. "I only just made up my mind this afternoon."

We'd barely gotten home when my mother and father stopped by to see "how you children are getting along." They brought us a portable television set with a stand which Bo Jo plugged in and turned on to a baseball game. While they were there, Bo Jo's parents came. His mother brought a sampler which she said had been stitched by Bo Jo's great-aunt a hundred years ago. It said *God Bless This Home,* and Bo Jo's mother said she thought it would look nice over the bookcase, and then she saw the new TV and turned red in the face and folded the sampler back into the tissue paper she'd taken it out of and put it on the dining room table.

It was the first time my father and Bo Jo's father had met face to face, which was a very uncomfortable feeling all around. Mr. Jones gave Father a once-over with his eyes, and Father gave Mr. Jones a brusque "How do you do" as though he remembered the face but had forgotten the name, and Mrs. Jones and Mother said in the same breath, "We only dropped in for a minute to see how the children are getting along."

I said, "Won't you sit down?"

There weren't enough chairs without pulling in two from the kitchen-dining area which were hard and narrow and straight and which Mr. and Mrs. Jones sat on. Father, after sending Mother a few S.O.S.'s with his eyes, which she pretended not to get, let himself down on the arm of the chair in which she was sitting. The chair was directly opposite the Joneses' two straight chairs, and the only way the two sets of parents could avoid looking at each other was to look at Bo Jo and me on the couch.

"The apartment is bigger than it seemed at first," Mother and Mrs. Jones said in the same breath.

"What did you say you pay for this?" Mr. Jones said.

"Forty-five dollars," Bo Jo said, and blushed. I suppose the blush was because he hadn't told his parents that my parents had put down the first month's rent as a wedding present. One of them. The television set was another.

"Remember the place we had, Fanny?" he said to Mrs. Jones. "Eighteen dollars and twice this size."

90

"But we had to share the bathroom," Mrs. Jones said, "with the Petersons. Remember?"

"I'll say. Never knew a man could spend so much time on—"

"Carson!" Mrs. Jones said, and blushed and my mother said to me as though she hadn't heard either of them,

"I think you'll find Hatty Barnes a dear. Especially if she likes you."

"What if she doesn't?"

"Oh, but she will. She adores young people. Your father says it is because she was never young herself . . . brought up by a maiden aunt."

"What's wrong with that?" Mr. Jones said.

"I beg your pardon?" Mother said. "With what?"

"With being brought up by your aunt!"

Father, who had been looking out of the window in a bored sort of way, said, "This was a *maiden* aunt."

"Oh," said Mr. Jones, and sat back in his chair.

"Did you go to church this morning?" Mrs. Jones asked Bo Jo.

"You know I hardly ever go to church."

"I thought what has happened might make a difference with your attitude."

"I hardly ever go to church," Bo Jo repeated, beginning to get red around the ears.

"That is something they will just have to work out for themselves," Mother said brightly, and got to her feet.

"I am an Episcopalian," Father said, as though that settled everything, and helped Mother into her coat.

"Sorry, dears," Mother said, "but Father and I have an engagement at five. . . ."

After they'd gone, there was the kind of silence that leaves everybody hanging. Bo Jo was brooding about his mother scolding him in front of my folks and I didn't blame him. There's nothing more humiliating than being treated like a kid in front of people for whom you're trying to be a man. And Mr. Jones was brooding about whatever it is he broods about when he isn't watching TV.

"Well," Bo Jo's mother said, "I guess we'd better run along too." I didn't protest though they'd hardly been there twenty minutes all told.

We scrounged up some supper out of the icebox, looked

at television a couple of hours and went to bed. Bo Jo went right to sleep, but all of a sudden I felt very strange about being here alone with Bo Jo. The light from Hatty Barnes' bedroom reflected in the mirror over the dresser. I was glad it was there. Like the night-light in my room when I was little and scared of the dark. I looked around trying to get used to where and how everything was, and when Hatty Barnes' light went out, I climbed over into Bo Jo's bed and went to sleep.

The whole gruesome time with Bo Jo's family I had been sure that moving into our own place would solve all of our problems. Or at least all of mine. But as long as I live I'll never forget what an eye-opener that first day alone in the apartment was.

It started out fine. Just like a television commercial taking the detergents out and leaving the young bride and groom playing house. Bo Jo looked grown-up and businesslike dressed for his job at the bank, and while I wasn't dressed, I'd brushed my hair and tied it on top of my head with a ribbon and put on lipstick and also some of the Patou eau de cologne Mother's Cousin Ellen brought me from Paris. We didn't have a newspaper so Bo Jo turned on the television to the news, and we discussed the high points. The bank was half an hour's walk away, but Bo Jo said he'd better allow forty-five minutes. He said the less important the job the more important it is to be on time. I went to the door with him and out on to the stoop. He kissed me and ran down the steps. On the corner a bunch of high school kids were waiting for the bus. They gave Bo Jo the big wave. There were probably some of them that thought he was going to catch the bus too. He waved back, but his wave wasn't very high or sweeping, and I couldn't help thinking that his hand, held out like that, looked like a flag at half-mast.

I went inside and bustled around making like a housewife, but to my absolute horror when I was finished, completely finished and nothing left to do, I looked at the clock and it was only ten A.M. and eight great big fat hours to fill up before Bo Jo would be home!

I tried telling myself that actually it was like a Saturday and I'd always adored Saturdays, but all that did was to

92

start me thinking about school and what period it was now.

I looked at part of a jackpot quiz program.

I then watched a soap opera until I remembered what my opinion was of women who sat around all day watching soap operas . . . namely Bo Jo's mother.

I then went into the bedroom and wound up the dancy doll powder box. Bo Jo's trombone was sitting in the chair like it owned the place, and I picked it up and tried to make a civilized sound come out of it.

I then went and looked out of the window down on Hatty Barnes' terrace, but nothing was stirring there.

I went to the front door and looked down on the street, but nothing was stirring there.

I went and stood in front of the bookcase, but everything in it I'd read a dozen times, which is why they were there. Part of another life, and I could no more go back to them right now than I could to it.

I wondered what other young brides found to do with themselves all day, but the only one I'd ever known was Tommy Ryan's older sister who'd married a lawyer and lived in an adorable house on Caper's Lane and led, it seemed to me now, a charmed life, raising poodles, playing tennis, golf and bridge the livelong day and coming home every night to roost on the young lawyer's lap in front of the fire in a white brick fireplace with brass andirons holding up the logs. They'd moved to Virginia, but even if they hadn't, she'd still probably think of me as an absolute infant . . . the little Greher girl, Tommy's high school chum.

I began to feel as though the apartment walls were closing in on me, and when I looked at the windows I could almost see the bars. I dashed out of the door and down the steps and across the garden to Hatty Barnes' back door and asked her if I could use her phone.

Hatty Barnes is plump and pretty and has oodles of money, and everybody in Trilby has a different theory about why she's never married.

There was a telephone in her kitchen, but the dryer was making such a racket she led me down the hall and into a kind of study where there was another one.

"Is everything in the apartment working properly?"

I said it was.

She said, "I suppose the only way to get married is when you're too young to know any better."

I blushed and she said, "I suppose you're going to have a baby." But she said it so matter-of-factly I couldn't get mad, but I couldn't think of anything to say either, and suddenly she smiled.

"Don't mind me, child. It's pure envy talking. It may seem to you now that life has you by the throat, but at least you know it's there. Life has never laid a hand on me, child. Not even a finger. Here's the phone book if you need it. And always feel free ... any time...." She trotted off and shut the door, and I dialed our house. I hoped Mother would ask me over for lunch or just ask me over.

She said, "Hello, darling. I'm so glad you called. I thought of running over, but Gory has been sent home from school with what may be a broken ankle so I'm taking him out to the hospital for X rays in a few minutes. How are you?"

"I'm sorry about Gory," I said.

"I know. It's always something. He's so careless with himself. . . ."

"Mother," I said, "when you were first married what did you do all day?"

"Do?" Mother said.

"With your time."

"That was so long ago I can hardly ... it seems to me there were parties, lots of parties, and ... Just a minute, Gory," she said to Gory, and to me, "I really must dash, darling. He's in a good deal of pain and . . ."

"I do hope it's just a sprain," I said.

"I'll let you know," Mother said.

I looked for Hatty Barnes on the way out. I had half a mind to ask her to come up to the apartment and have lunch with me, but I couldn't imagine what she'd make of it. The idea that she might make the truth of it ... that after two weeks and two days of marriage I was bored silly and lonesome as a polecat ... made me give up the notion.

I went up to the apartment and looked in the icebox, but I wasn't hungry. I got a glass of milk and a box of

94

cookies and went and turned on television, and hating myself, watched three soap operas in a row.

By that time it was almost time to start cooking supper.

By that time it was almost time for Bo Jo to come home.

It was wonderful having it almost time for something.

Yet when Bo Jo asked me what I'd been doing with myself all day I found myself babbling on as though I'd been busy as the proverbial bee. Covering up. The worst of it was I couldn't see that tomorrow was going to be any different. But it was. That was the day I met Lou Consuela. Mrs. Nicolas Consuela, to be exact. We met in the supermarket. I noticed her at first because there was something familiar about her. I was almost sure I had seen her somewhere before. She was skinny and dark with a thick black ponytail. She didn't look much more than sixteen, and she was wearing a wedding ring. I noticed all these things while we were both picking over potatoes at the vegetable counter. I didn't think she noticed me, but out of the blue she said, "Hey, that spud you just put in your bag has a spot on it as big as a dollar."

I looked in my bag, and she reached across me and dove her hand in and pulled out a potato with sure enough a spot on it as big as a dollar.

I said, "Gee, thanks. I didn't even see it."

"New at this business, aren't you?"

"Yes," I said. "But then so are you, aren't you?"

"Not at pinching pennies and finding the rotten spots in things." She smiled a crooked smile. "But being married, yes. Eight months tomorrow. What's your score?"

"About two weeks."

"You *are* a bride!" She looked me over scowling. "About seventeen?"

"Almost," I said.

"I'll be eighteen next month," she said. "But I'm old for my age. Always have been."

Maybe she was, but she didn't look it, not with that ponytail and red culottes and red scuffy sandals.

"Have you lived in Trilby long?" I said.

"Like a hundred years! Six months to be exact. And you?"

"All my life," I said.

"Poor kid," she said, and moved on down to the lemons. I didn't need lemons, but I followed her and put a couple of lemons in a bag. "I'm out of Chicago," she said. "Now there's a town. If I'd thought Nick, that's my husband, was going to leave it I'd have thought twice I can tell you!"

"Trilby is small," I said. "But maybe when you get used to it—"

"That's what I'm fighting!" she interrupted. "I don't want to get used to it. I've got ambition." Suddenly she looked at me and smiled. When she smiled she was very pretty. Her dark eyes sparkled and her cheeks dimpled. "But why take it out on you?" she said. "How about stopping off at our pad for a cup of coffee on your way home? It's only a couple of blocks away."

I'd been wondering how to prolong the conversation. I said I'd love to. She had some more shopping to do so I waited for her outside. When she came out she was frowning.

"I think I got gypped on the steak," she said. "How much is three times eighty-nine?"

"Two sixty-seven, I think."

"I knew it! I've a mind to go right back and . . ." She shrugged. "Oh, well, what's four cents? I just hate to have anyone think they can put anything over on me. Don't you?"

"I don't know," I said. "I never count up. I just take it for granted they're right."

"You *are* a baby," she said. "Incidentally, the name is Lou. Louella Consuela. How's that for a handle?"

"Sounds as though it should be in lights somewhere," I said.

"Over a nightclub," she said. "One of these small cozy places that you can't get out of for under fifty bucks, and the people come just to hear *you*. That's the thought. One of these days . . ."

I remembered then where I had seen her before. The Reef in Savannah the night we were celbrating Bo Jo's scholarship . . . the ladies' room at the Reef and Brahms' Lullaby, which she'd sung to her own words. . . .

"I heard you one night," I said, "at the Reef. Have you had any other theatrical experience?"

96

"Second line of the chorus is all. Two Chicago openings. One flopped after four nights, but the other was slated for Broadway."

"You didn't go?"

"No, I didn't go. Nick said marry him. Choose. Now or never. I figured show business would always be there, and he wouldn't, not the way women go for him. I must have been out of my mind."

"You were probably in love with him," I said.

"You can say *that* again!" Lou said. "Well, here we are."

We had turned in at a shingled bungalow on Wren Street. It was a neighborhood that I was familiar with on account of Mrs. Boone, who does Mother's sewing. She lives there. It was a street of shabby bungalows and great huge old trees and proud tidy little plots of grass and flowers. Only there weren't, I noticed, any flowers in front of Lou's house.

"Gloomy, isn't it?" She heisted her packages onto her hip so she could open the front door. "But I can't kick. We could have had a cottage out at the farm, dishwasher and all, but I said nix to the country. At least here when I get stir crazy I can put on the glad rags and go and sit in the hotel bar and play games."

"Games?"

"Don't sound so shocked! With myself. Like say it's the Palmer House and I'm waiting for Richard Burton."

She shoved through the door and I behind her.

"Wanta wait in here while I instant up some coffee?"

"In here" was a big bare room with a big square, armless, backless sofa right in the middle of it, a piano against one wall and a homemade stereo against the other. There was an open fireplace with an outdoor steak grill sitting in it, a glass-topped coffee table covered with record albums, sheet music, filled ashtrays, empty glasses and various magazines, among them an old copy of *Town and Country*. The walls were white except for the end wall, which was obviously freshly painted a bright blue and was covered with tacked-up photographs of horses, of Lou in leotards with arms circled above her head and toe pointed outward, of Lou in evening dress singing into a microphone, of a dark handsome man wearing riding pants and a sombrero. I wanted to ask Lou if he was her husband, but she'd already disappeared.

She was back in a minute with an empty tray and scooped up the dirty ashtrays and glasses.

"Company last night," she said. "Stayed until two A.M. Old jockey buddy of Nick's." Before I could ask any questions she was gone again. This time I followed her into the kitchen.

"Would you like to put your perishables in my icebox until you go?" she said.

"Perishables?"

"Butter, eggs, meat . . ."

"I don't have any," I said, and tried not to peer around too obviously. I think the two things in a person's house that tell you the most about them are the medicine cabinet and the icebox—what is in them, I mean. Lou's icebox, except for the groceries she was now putting in it, was almost empty except for some cans of beer, a bottle of olives, a bottle of milk, a half empty tin of sardines, and one cold gray hamburger patty. The room had two windows but no curtains, a table but no chairs, a light bulb with no shade that hung down from the ceiling, and if it weren't for the sink which was full of dirty dishes you'd think they'd just moved in that morning. The kettle began to scream, and she slammed the icebox door and reached for some cups from a shelf.

"You said something about a farm," I said. "Is your husband a farmer?"

"Him?" She burst out laughing. Her laugh was like a scale running backwards. "Sorry, You'd have no way of knowing, not having met him but that's the last thing, the very last . . . He's a trainer. Of horses. Thoroughbreds. He's at Braithwaite Farms. To hear him tell it you'd think it was Calumet, but it is a step up. Ever heard of Lancelot II out of Naomi?"

"No. But I do know about Braithwaite Farms. I guess just about everybody knows about that. I've been out there with my father. He . . ." I'd been about to say that my father's bank had handled the sale of Oak Point Plantation to the New York financier who wanted it for his racehorses, that I'd met Mr. Braithwaite, but I realized

98

maybe it would sound as though I were trying to impress her, so I said, "It must be very interesting work."

"He likes it. So that makes me stuck with it. Cream or sugar?"

"Both," I said.

She handed me my cup and started out of the room. "Kitchens give me claustrophobia," she said. "Do you like housework?"

"I don't know yet," I said. "At least it gives me something to do."

"Something to do!" In the living room Lou grabbed a pillow off the sofa, dropped it on the floor and sat down on it. I got another pillow and did the same, crossing my legs under me. "Holy one-eyed snails," Lou said. "You must be hard up for entertainment if housework is the answer."

"Well," I said, "what is there to do when you come right down to it? What do *you* do all day?"

"Oh, I keep busy." She paused and thought a minute. "I sleep late for one thing. And I practice every day." She indicated the sheet music, the piano, the stereo, with a sweep of her hand. "Song and dance numbers ... and there are some TV shows on in the afternoon I wouldn't miss for the world. And, like I said, when I go stir crazy I go to the hotel and sit in the bar."

"Your husband doesn't mind?"

"Mind? He'd kill me if he knew! He'd get all the wrong ideas. The most I ever have is a glass of sherry. I just go for the atmosphere. I find it necessary to me. He'd never understand that."

"He's older than you, isn't he?" I was looking at the picture of the man in the sombrero.

"Twenty-seven next week," she said. "Good-looking son of a gun, isn't he? How old's yours?"

"Seventeen," I said and blushed, sure that would tell her everything, but if it did she didn't show it.

"What does he do?" she said.

"Works in a bank. Greher Guaranty and Trust."

"La-de-da!" she said.

"It's not like that at all," I said. "He runs a computing machine."

"You know, I don't even know your name. . . ."

"July. July Jones."

"Cute."

"I was born on the Fourth of July, and my parents got carried away with the idea."

"What's *your* husband like?"

"Bo Jo? Well, he's—"

"Holy stubbed-tail cats! Is it *really* Bo Jo?"

"It's really Boswell Johnson. Boswell Johnson Jones."

"You and he get along all right?" She scrambled up off her cushion, went and got a fresh pack of cigarettes and sat down again.

"Goodness," I said, "how should I know after only two weeks! Do you always ask such personal questions?"

"I don't know," she said. "It's been so long since I've had anybody to ask questions, I mean anybody anywhere near my age with the same marital status. All of our friends are really Nick's friends, horse people, and years older ... the women treat me as though I were some kind of Lolita, and the men ignore me on account of Nick would knock them cold if they didn't. So," she spread her hands out and shrugged, "when I saw you at the super-market this morning wearing a wedding ring yet, I felt like I'd struck oil."

"I felt the same," I said, "seeing you."

"But you've lived here all your life. You must have oodles of friends."

"I don't have any married friends," I said. "Not one. And my being married makes a difference with the friends I've got. I've noticed it already."

"Nothing in common," Lou said.

"Not a thing," I said.

"It's a different world."

"And I'm not even sure I like it," I blurted, and then sort of laughed. "There you are," I said. "I could never have said that to Mary Ann, and I've known her practi-cally all my life."

"What don't you like? The going to bed bit?" Lou said. Just like it could have been the cooking bit or the washing bit or the ironing bit.

"I didn't mean that at *all*," I said, somewhat shocked.

"Well, you'd be amazed at how many women don't. It

100

even took me awhile, and I'd always considered myself the passionate type."

The truth was it scared me that when Bo Jo made love to me I just wasn't with it after a certain point. After a certain point I felt as though he went off somewhere and forgot I was even there. It scared me that just when I shoud be feeling closest to him I felt farther away than ever. But I didn't even like to think about it, much less talk about it.

"What I meant," I said, "was that I wasn't sure I liked being in a different world from everybody else my age."

"Oh, you'll make your own world pretty soon. Just like I have."

I stayed on for another cup of coffee and looked at her high school annual and the scrapbook she'd started keeping when she got her first singing job in Chicago. When I left I asked her to come and have lunch with me the next day, and she said she'd love to.

That very afternoon Mary Ann dropped in on her way home from school. It was the first time she'd seen the apartment, the first time we'd been alone together since I got married, and I felt as strange and uncomfortable with her as if I'd never known her before. She dumped her books down on the dining table and looked around.

"What an adorable place," she said. "How I do envy you. If only Alan and I . . ."

Which she didn't mean for a minute. I was sure she was madly in love with Alan, but the house parties at Bowers, the dances, the planning, the waiting, the recipe collecting, and domestic science courses meant just as much to her as being in love, and I knew she wouldn't want to be in my shoes for a million dollars. But I realized she was trying to be nice and probably felt just as strange with me as I did with her.

"The bedroom and bath are over there," I said, and she went and peeked in the bedroom and quickly backed out again looking as flustered as if she'd stumbled on Bo Jo undressed, which wasn't possible because he was at the bank.

"Just adorable," she said again and then, I guess, just to prove she wasn't embarrassed, she said breezily, "But I

101

thought everybody had a double bed when they first got married."

"Miss Hatty Barnes decides that," I said. "Practically everything in here is hers. How about a snack?"

"Marvelous." She came and looked over my shoulder into the icebox. "Remember how we used to always raid the icebox after school?"

Remember? That had been a bare two weeks ago! "Just like old times!" I said. "Like long ago when we were young." I doubled over and pretended to walk with a cane.

"Well, it does *seem* ages," Mary Ann said, and blushed. Sometimes she has no sense of humor. "I mean actually you and Bo Jo have literally skipped over whole years of life just as though they weren't there. It gives the rest of us a queer feeling."

"What do you think it gives us?" I said, and got out Cokes and a jar of peanut butter and some bread.

"I might as well be frank," Mary Ann said, and flipped the top off the Cokes against the handle of the cabinet door, and now she really was blushing, "but I honestly don't understand it." She is very fair and when she blushes it's as though she's running a high and dangerous fever.

She was certainly asking for it, and I supposed I might as well let her have it as she'd find out sooner or later.

"I think you do," I said, and slapped inches of peanut butter onto the bread slices.

"Well, naturally there's been a lot of irresponsible yack around school like there always is when somebody gets married like that ... people like Alicia Helms ... you know she was pretty crazy about Bo Jo ... but your true friends know better."

"Just what is Alicia saying?" I sat down at the table and wolfed into my sandwich. I always wolf food when I'm upset.

"The usual," Mary Ann said, "what unkind people usually say when somebody runs off and gets married." She was practically stammering, and I felt sorry for her. "But I told her it was just sour grapes on her part. I told her right to her face with half a dozen people to hear me."

"You shouldn't have," I said, and got up and began

102

making another sandwich, which I needed like a hole in the head as the first one was making a knot in my stomach.

"Well, I did," Mary Ann said, not looking at me.

"Well, you shouldn't have," I said, not looking at her.

"I don't think you *realize* what it was she said."

"Oh, Mary Ann, I'm not that stupid! What do you want—a signed confession? So yes we *had* to get married."

"This peanut butter is sticking in my throat," Mary Ann said. "Don't you have something slippery like jelly?"

I got out a jar of marmalade. "You didn't think I'd do anything like that without a *reason,* did you? I'm not that immature."

"Nooo," Mary Ann said, "but then I didn't think you would do the other. I mean, it scares me. It actually scares me . . . you of all people . . . you always seemed so clever and sure of yourself . . ."

"So all right, I'm a loose and wanton person, but please let's skip the sermon." I don't know why I was so hurt. I hadn't expected her to be anything *but* shocked.

"You don't understand," her voice sounded as though it had tears in it, "it's not you I'm thinking about. But me. Alan and me. It scares me about us. . . ."

"It shouldn't," I said crossly, "this could never happen to you and Alan. You're, you're different."

"That's what scares me," Mary Ann said. "I wish I could think you were just all those things you said and be shocked and feel superior and let it go at that. Instead my whole entire point of view is knocked for a loop, and I don't know what to think. I mean Alan and I have been in love, or thought we were, for almost two years, and it has never occurred to either of us not to wait until . . . It makes me wonder if . . . if . . . well, if he is really as crazy in love as he says, and . . . and . . . what I would do if he ever really wanted me to bad enough—" She wheeled up from the table and went into the living room. "You do have a record player, don't you? How about some glad noise for a change?"

"The records," I said, "are under the bookcase."

I knew she'd put on a Belafonte, one of the gay, soft ones, and she did. I felt simply terrible. Alan was the only

103

secure thing that had ever happened to Mary Ann. All she'd had until he came along was a steady turnover of mothers and stepmothers and half brothers and sisters and noisy divorces.

I thought about this as I cleaned up the kitchen. When I went into the living room she was sitting on the sofa looking down onto Hatty Barnes' terrace.

"She's having tea," Mary Ann said, "with Preacher Dobbs. I hear he's courting her. She'll never marry him, but I wonder why she never has married. . . ."

It was an easy out. A good topic of conversation. I could go over and look out the window too and talk about Hatty Barnes until it was time for Mary Ann to go home. It would save me a lot of humiliation and maybe once she got home and thought it over she'd see it all differently. But then again she might not.

I said, "Look, don't get the wrong impression. I mean this thing with Bo Jo and me, this thing between us . . . whatever it was that happened it . . . it . . . wasn't because we or maybe he, was so much in love we, he, couldn't help it. If he, we, had been it probably wouldn't have. . . . Bo Jo isn't in love with me, Mary Ann. Not the way Alan is with you. That's why it's never been any problem for you. Alan loves you. Truly. Enough to . . . enough not to . . ."

She looked at me startled and looked away again, out of the window. "You wouldn't make a thing like that up just to . . . I mean, it would be a terrible thing to say if it weren't true. . . ." She looked back, a big unhappy question mark in her eyes.

"It is a terrible thing to say," I said, "and it is true. We don't feel about each other the way you and Alan do. Not even close. . . ."

"How horrible!" she said. "How dreadful for you."

"Oh, it's not *that* horrible. It's just different with us."

"Then this is all sort of temporary? Until you have the baby?"

For a minute I didn't know what she meant. I thought maybe she meant the apartment . . . that it wouldn't be big enough after the baby came. When I realized it wasn't the apartment she was talking about but our marriage, I was shocked.

104

"Of course not," I said. "After all, a marriage is a marriage whatever the reasons for it. I mean you make certain promises." But even while I was spouting off I was thinking that maybe everyone was thinking just what Mary Ann thought, maybe everyone was counting on it. My parents. Bo Jo's parents. Even Bo Jo. The idea froze me.

"One thing at a time," I said to Mary Ann. "That's as far as I can think."

"I'm terribly sorry," Mary Ann said, but she was calm again and wore the preoccupied serene look she always gets when she is thinking about Alan and pretty soon she left.

That night I didn't tell Bo Jo about Mary Ann's visit but I did tell him about Lou's. I thought he'd be pleased that I had made a new friend. But he wasn't. Not when he found out who she was.

"She's not your type," he said.

"How on earth can you tell? You hardly know her. In fact, you don't really. Not nearly as well as I do."

"Instant friendship!" Bo Jo sneered.

"I didn't say that. I only said from what I've seen of her I like her. At least she's going to do something with her life."

"Such as?"

"Show business. She practices every day."

"I didn't think what she had to offer at the Reef was so hot."

"Everybody else did. Actually I think you did too only you won't admit it now."

"That's not so. If there's one thing I know it's music!"

This great declaration all on the basis of Ta Ra Ra Boom De-Ay on the trombone! I had to smile. I couldn't help it, and I'm sure if Charlie Saunders hadn't come busting in the front door just then Bo Jo would have gone slamming out of it.

"Fighting already?" said Charlie, and went up and slapped Bo Jo on the back as though he hadn't seen him in years. Whereupon Bo Jo slapped him on the back about six times, both of them grinning like fools. It was the first time any of our friends had come to the apartment but still it seemed to me a lot of fuss to be making over it.

When they'd finished with the slapping bit, Charlie looked around at everything. "Not bad. Not bad. Alicia's down in the car. She didn't want to come up until I'd checked." He winked at Bo Jo. "Didn't want to walk in on anything."

"Aw, cut it," Bo Jo said. "Bring her on up."

She was, of course, the last person I wanted to see. Also we'd been so busy talking about Lou Consuela that I hadn't even started supper. In fact, I hadn't even planned it. When Charlie went down to get Alicia, I said to Bo Jo, "I simply can't ask them for supper. I've never cooked for more than two people in my life."

"Don't cook. Just give them what you usually give me. Sandwiches, canned soup, potato chips . . ."

"I can't," I wailed. "It would be all over school by tomorrow."

"Brides aren't supposed to know anything about cooking. That's what all the corny jokes are about."

"I don't want to be a joke. Not when Alicia's around."

"Oh, for Pete's sake!"

"Well, you were crazy about her once! And she's still crazy about you." The minute I said it I knew from the surprised, pleased look on Bo Jo's face that I'd made a mistake.

"What makes you think that?" He really wanted to know.

"I could be wrong," I said, and shrugged. Bo Jo started to say something, but we could hear their voices on the outside stairs so we both clammed up.

They stayed and stayed. We tried to wait them out but I began to feel positively weak and I could hear Bo Jo's stomach growling all the way across the room. I hoped Alicia could hear it too. We finally ended by going, the four of us, to the Coffee Pot and spending next Sunday's movie money as well as three dollars we'd put aside for "an emergency."

After all that, I could hardly believe my ears when in the car coming home I heard Bo Jo say, "Why don't you come up for a nightcap? I think we've got a couple of Cokes, haven't we, July?"

106

We had a whole wretched carton of them. "Yes," I said, "why don't you?"

Of course they did. Alicia draped herself out full length on the couch, yawning that she was tired from some party she'd been to the night before. She has about the prettiest legs I've even seen and almost perfect bosoms. I couldn't bear to look at her. We played some records and watched *The Man from U.N.C.L.E.* Finally they left. I'd planned when we got in bed to have it out about Alicia and about Charlie, who would probably be dropping in all the time now that he'd found it so cozy, and about the money we'd spent at the Coffee Pot, but I was too tired by then to battle and the next morning when I woke up it didn't seem all that important.

As it turned out, Gory's sprain was a lulu. I went over the next morning to play checkers with him while Mother did her marketing.

I rather dreaded being alone with Gory. We hadn't been alone since I got married. In spite of the cookbook I wasn't sure how he was feeling about me these days and if I were alone with him for five minutes I knew I was bound to find out. Even if he manages to keep his feelings from spilling out of his mouth they spill out of his face.

He was propped up on the sofa on the sun porch, soaking the ankle in warm water and Epsom salts. He was working on one of his model planes. He looked cross and preoccupied.

"How's the foot?" I said cheerily.

"How's the foot, how's the foot, how's the foot! That's all I hear. The foot's just fine but they won't let me *do* anything. Not ride my bike. Not walk from here to Pete's even. Nothing."

"How about a game of checkers?"

"I'm sick of checkers."

"Monopoly then?"

"I'm sick of that too."

"You are in a mood. Maybe you'd rather I just went home."

"Aw, for cripes sake, for cripes sake . . ."

"Well, I have got better things to do with my time than

107

sit around watching you build model planes." Just what those better things were I did not know.

"Whadja have to go and get married for?"

I couldn't tell whether he asked the question just out of crossness or if the crossness was because of the question.

"Don't tell me you actually miss me?" I teased, stalling for time.

"You haven't gone anywhere yet. What's a few blocks away?"

What indeed! "Then why don't you ever come to see me?" I said.

"I started to once." His lips clamped shut and he looked away.

"Why didn't you?"

"I dunno."

"You mad at me, Gory?"

"No. At him. Bo Jo."

Maybe I should have let it drop there, but I didn't.

"Why?"

"I hate him, that's why." And I believed him. It glittered from his eyes and turned his cheeks pale.

Nothing that Mother or Father had ever said or intimated to me about their disapproval of Bo Jo had hurt me like this did. Gory, who had never hated anything or anyone in his life. What was it Reverend Michael had said of him—"He was born with a gift for loving"—and I had known this to be true. I had seen it in his devotion to our parents and felt it in his affection for me.

"Oh no, you mustn't," I said, meaning not so much that he mustn't hate Bo Jo but that he mustn't be changed by what had happened.

"I've heard Mother and Father talking, and I hate him," he repeated, and picked up his jackknife and began to whittle at a piece of wood.

Again I should have let it drop.

"What did they say?" I said.

"They said he's put a baby inside you!" He looked up then, his cheeks blazing with shame. I wanted to slap him. "Is it true?" he said.

"It's none of your business," I said, "or theirs. It's nobody's business but Bo Jo's and mine, do you hear!

108

And next time you hear them talking you tell them so!" The tears were pouring down my cheeks in a dead giveaway.

He was staring at me with a kind of blank and puzzled look like he'd never seen me before and I guess, like this, he never had. Seeing that blank stare and the cowlick sprouting up from his forehead and the freckles beginning to show through the red again, I remembered he was just a kid. My little brother. I felt terrible. I swiped at my eyes with the back of my hand.

"Look," I said, "are we going to play checkers or aren't we? Because if we're not I'm going to run along."

"Sure, we're going to play. I just had to get this wing tip glued was all." His hands bustled about setting up the men on the board while I drew up a chair and made his propped leg more comfortable. "And you don't have to *let* me win. I can even beat Father now," he said.

We were almost back to normal when Mother returned from her errands, but even so, I was awfully glad to see her come back. She brought me a letter from the post office in a handwriting I was not familiar with. It was air mail from California.

Mother said, "I didn't know you had friends in California."

I said, "Neither did I." But faintly a bell was ringing and it had to do with the nephew the Clarks had brought around the night Bo Jo and I were married, so I put the letter in my pocket unopened.

"Incidentally," Mother said, "I've made an appointment for you to see Dr. Pearless on Wednesday at ten. I wish Dr. Wilson were still alive, but we've heard splendid things about Dr. Pearless . . . he delivered Myrt Hollings' twins . . . I think you'll like him."

I had already talked to Bo Jo about Dr. Pearless, and Bo Jo had asked around and found out that he charged twice as much as anyone else in town. I said, "We can't afford Dr. Pearless. We're thinking about Dr. Harvey."

"I've never heard of him," Mother said, as though that settled it.

"He's new," I said. "Just out of medical school."

"Please," Mother said, "we want someone who is experienced, someone we can completely depend on. Money should be no consideration in a matter as important as this one. It was manful and thoughtful of Bo Jo to want to keep expenses down, but this is something we want to do for you."

"I don't think Bo Jo realized that," I said.

"Well, you may tell him . . . doctor, hospital, all medical expenses."

"You're much too good to me," I said, and hugged her gratefully.

I didn't open the letter from California until I got back to the apartment. It was from the Clarks' nephew. Horace. Horace Clark. His name and address was at the top of the page.

DEAR JULY,

What a marvelous name! White sails, blue skies, warm nights, fireworks, and the Star-Spangled Banner!

Meeting you was the best thing that's happened to me lately. Seems as though I've known you forever. Sometimes it's like that with people. And it's not only because you're a GIRL and I'm a BOY, though I'm very happy that that is so.

What are your summer plans? I am going to be working. My honorable pater is putting me to work as a riveter in an aircraft plant. It pays better than vice-president and will, he hopes, make a MAN of me. He comes from a long line of MEN and doesn't know what to make of a son who flops around all day reading books and scribbling.

I forgot to ask . . . do you like poetry? And I don't mean all those espresso boys crying into their beards. I am speaking of the gusty, clearheaded, wholehearted singers of verses—Whitman, Kipling, Coleridge, etc.???

School has seemed hellishly flat since I got back. Partly because I'm already thinking in terms of Princeton next fall, but there is another BIG reason which you may learn by sending a letter and self-addressed envelope to Horace B. Clark at the address at the top of this page. I'll sit right here and not move until I hear from you.

Yours,
HORACE

I'd had snow letters from boys before and mash notes from boys in school but this, I knew, was different. Excitingly different. This was no schoolboy, this was a junior in college, who liked to talk about the same things I did. Who was interested in my mind. I also knew what I must do about it and right away before I was tempted to do anything else.

There was no stationery in the apartment—that was one of those things we hadn't gotten around to—so I found a notebook that I'd used in school and sat down at the dining room table and wrote very fast so as not to change my mind. I wrote:

DEAR HORACE,

Thank you very much for your nice letter. I am very happy for you that you got into Princeton and hope it will be all that you expect. I too have made a transfer you might say . . . a very happy one. I am now married to a wonderful boy and expect to live, as the saying goes, happily ever after.

Best of luck to you,
JULY JONES

I erased a smudge where a tear had plopped on, of all places, the word "happily" and was about to put it in an envelope when I heard someone climbing the outside steps and there was Lou come for lunch which in the excitement of getting the letter I'd forgotten all about.

"I hope I'm not interrupting anything," she said.

"Not at all," I said, and jumped up guiltily. The letter to Horace slid to the floor and before I saw it I had stepped on it. I picked it up and looked at it. It was soiled. Ruined. I scrunched it up and threw it into the wastebasket.

Lou looked different today. She was wearing heels and a tight-fitting navy dress which showed off her pointed bosoms and narrow waist. Her hair was done up in a coil on top of her head and on top of the coil was a tiny bit of black lace, a minute mantilla which I guessed passes for a hat.

When she saw me looking at her, she said, "This isn't my usual lunch with a pal outfit. I've just come from a wedding. At Saint Mark's. The bride was so ugly that even yards and yards of tulle didn't help, but the church was lovely . . . all those spring flowers . . . and the groom was a living doll. What's she got? Money?"

"That must have been the Tupper wedding," I said. "Do you know them?"

"Until today they were just names in the paper—Nancy Gardner Tupper and Roger DeVries. I like to go to weddings, that's all. Funerals too. I identify. It's better than reading a book. Do you like provolone?"

She was carrying, I saw then, a brown paper bag which she began emptying on the table, salami, cheese, some oranges, and a pastry.

"This was to be *my* lunch," I said.

"I know. But I just happened to pass a delicatessen. Or not to pass it. Getting me by a delicatessen is like trying to get a dog past a fire hydrant." She wandered into the living room, looked out of the window. "A terrace yet! This is an 'in' neighborhood all right. And would you look at that garden with the hedge around it and all the little pebble paths. What do you pay for this joint?"

I told her and she shook her head. "And we pay sixty for the cave."

"Do you actually *read* all this literature?" She stood in front of the bookcase scowling. "The titles read like some sort of required school list. Maybe it's your husband who's the bookworm. . . ."

"He's more interested in sports," I said.

"Bleak House," she said, *"Dodsworth, Wuthering Heights . . ."* Most of these have been in pictures . . . what I do is wait until they make a picture. If a book is good enough they always make a picture. Did you see *Saints and Sinners* from the book of that same name?"

"No," I said.

"Terrific!" she said. "Absolutely terrific," she said, and came and sat down at the table and bit into an orange. "It was about this girl that couldn't stand it because she had
112

only one life to live so she pretended to be four different women . . . and for a long time she got away with it. Her poor husband and the man whose mistress she was and her director and her rich husband—none of them knew the others existed until she got pregnant, and then you can just imagine!"

"Who did she choose?"

"The father of the baby natch. Isn't that always how it goes?"

"Did she know which one was?"

"Oh sure. They showed a love scene between her and her rich husband with a calendar hanging from a wall and the camera moving in on it. So from that you're supposed to guess. Of course, if I'd been in her shoes I'd have put the baby up for adoption and gone my merry way."

"That's what you think now," I said. "When it happens to you—"

"It's not going to happen to me!" She flushed angrily. "Not at *least* for five years. Not until I've had my fling at show business. Nick promised me . . . it was the one thing I made him promise before we ever bought the license."

"I'm sorry," I said. "I didn't know I was striking a nerve."

"It's the one thing I've got a horror of. Being tied to a brat before I've had time to live a little. It's a thing with me. Later, a long time from now—" She broke off and jumped up and walked into the living room and bent over the bookshelf where the records were. "Jeeze," she said. "Long-haired books and long-haired music. Do you have any Rosemary Clooney?"

She stayed until Bo Jo got home, and I never did have a chance to rewrite the letter to Horace. And by the next morning I didn't want to write it. By the next morning I felt entirely different about a lot of things. The fight with Bo Jo started over Lou. She'd hardly got out of the door before he said,

"Is *that* your supermarket pickup?" I suppose if I'd been older and more experienced I would have seen that he was tired and in a bad mood because of something that had happened at work, but I took it personally.

"She is my new friend," I said, "if that's what you mean. And I find her most interesting."

"Interesting? What's so interesting about her? She looks like just plain trouble to me. Bored and restless, just plain trouble. And frankly I don't see what you two have in common."

"Maybe I'm bored and restless," I said nastily. "Maybe I'm just plain trouble. I should think you'd be glad I'd found someone to talk to. I was about to go bug house up here alone all day every day."

"Poor little you," Bo Jo said, and stomped over and turned on the news. It was getting to be a habit, turning on the TV in the middle of an argument. I went over and turned it off.

I said, "You have no conception of what it's like having nothing to do all day. But I haven't complained. I haven't let on. I just went out and found myself a friend. Someone I can talk to, someone with maybe the same problems I've got."

"There's plenty you could be doing," Bo Jo said. "Like learning to cook something besides hamburgers for one thing, like learning to sew for another. Ma offered to teach you, but you gave her the brush-off."

"I hate sewing," I said, "I'd rather scrub floors."

"Then scrub them," Bo Jo said, and turned on the TV again. That was the last straw.

"I also hate being married!" I shouted above the announcer.

Bo Jo whirled around and stuck his face into mine and began shouting too.

"*You* hate marriage! How the hell do you think I react? I land my folks a punch they'll never get over. Give up school. College. Football. Everything down the drain. Trot to the damned bank every morning. Pull a damned lever all day. Trot back here at night. Back to what? That's what I want to know. Back to where? And *you* don't like being married. Well, that's just too God damned bad!" He flung around and slammed out of the front door. I ran after him howling that I was sorry, that I hadn't meant it, but he never turned around and by the time he hit the street he was running. I wasn't sure he'd ever come back.

I turned off the oven where I was baking potatoes and threw myself down on the couch and cried. I cried about everything bad that had happened from the time I was born until that night. It took until ten P.M As soon as I stopped crying I began being scared. I'd never been alone in a place all night. I began hearing things. Scratchy noises at the window and things on the roof.

When it got to be midnight I turned off the lights in the living room and turned on the light in the bedroom and went to bed. It was about two when he came in. He thumped through the living room turning on all the lights. I heard the icebox door open and shut and a little while after that he came into the bedroom. I shut my eyes and pretended I was asleep. He came and leaned over my bed, smelling revoltingly of beer.

He said, "Do you know where I've been?" He waited a minute and when I didn't say anything he said, "Are you asleep?" and sat down on the side of my bed. I didn't answer, and he said, "The fact is I've been drinking.

"The fact is," he said, "I've been drinking with the boys and—" he hiccoughed softly—"with the girls. I have, in fact, been out on the town. Free. Unchained."

He got up and began dropping off his clothes. At least that's what it sounded like; my eyes were still shut.

"When they asked me my name know what I told them? I told them my name was 'Mud.' I said just call me 'Mud.' " He laughed. I think it was a laugh. "Just call me Mud, I said."

He thumped across the room and fell onto his bed. "And when the bartender asked me how old I was I told him I was old enough to know Better. I asked him if he knew Better. I said Better was quite a guy ... *when* you got to know him. I'm a card," he said very slowly, "a real card," he said, and didn't say anything more. Pretty soon I squinted my eyes open. The light was still on. He was fast asleep on his back. And he didn't look as if he had a trouble in the world. I felt very bitter about this, his sleeping while I couldn't. I felt my tummy to see if there was any change there. It seemed to me I could feel a tightening of the skin over my abdomen. I wished the baby would hurry and grow big enough so that I could feel it when it moved. I needed some sort of proof of its existence more real than Bo Jo and I scratching each other's eyes out in Hatty Barnes' garage apartment.

I don't think Bo Jo remembered too much about that night. The next morning he had a preoccupied expression as though he were trying to put together a puzzle in his head. He said he was sorry and I said I was sorry, but we didn't look at each other when we said it and as soon as he was gone, I sat down and wrote a different letter to Horace Clark from the one I'd planned to write.

I wrote:

DEAR HORACE,

I simply adored your letter. It came at a time when I was feeling somewhat low, and it picked me right up. A riveter, yet? It sounds rough but you should pick up a lot of ideas for your "scribbling," as you call it. I mean rubbing elbows with LIFE every single day. I think I envy you.

"Yes" to do I like poetry. I even sometimes try to write it. And somewhat "No" to do I like Whitman Coleridge, Kipling, etc. Maybe I'm just not intellectual enough to appreciate them, but frankly Whitman leaves me cold. He's so blustery and full of himself and Coleridge, I think, is tiresome and lugubrious and Kipling . . . well, I do love his stories even if I don't go for his poetry. My favorites are Byron, Keats, Shelley, Amy Lowell, the Shakesperian sonnets . . . I guess you might say the romanticists. However, I couldn't agree with you more about the espresso boys. They are so gruesomely self-centered and undisciplined. I think poetry should have *some* discipline, don't you? I mean, even if it's free verse. You can't just run off the page. That's where the espresso boys go crazy. A friend of mine has a record that was taped in a San Francisco coffee house, and it's almost as far out as you can get without falling into outer space.

Goodness, how I do run on. But it's your fault for getting me started.

Good luck on your job and congratulations on Princeton.

I hesitated a long time over how to sign it. Sincerely yours was out as was Truly yours or anything pertaining to "yours." I finally just wrote my name at the bottom, my

116

first name only. I read it over once and couldn't honestly see anything wrong about sending it. It hardly read like a letter at all . . . more like a paper for English II. I put it in an envelope and addressed it and put it in Miss Hatty Barnes' mailbox for the postman to pick up.

That was only the beginning of our correspondence. It got to be a game with me, seeing how much I could tell him without telling him the facts. It meant writing a first draft and then copying it to make sure I'd not leaked anything. . . . Almost like writing for English II . . . challenging. Also it was fun. Like taking a short vacation from reality. And his letters to me were reward enough. I kept all of them. His letters and the first drafts of the ones I wrote in return. I kept them in the bottom tray of my jewelry box in my top bureau drawer, of all places. Bo Jo could have chanced on them any time he went looking for a safety pin and of course eventually did. Subconsciously I must have wanted him to. At the time, that is. When it finally did happen it was too late to do us any good and I wished it hadn't.

I have the letters here and just for the record . . . though they don't give much of a picture of my life during that period a few quotations from some of them might not be out of order as actually they themselves became a very important part of my life . . . my interior life, that is . . . at that time. . . .

July to Horace May 19th:

". . . there are some days that make you feel as though if you take too deep a breath you'll be lifted straight off the ground and into the air just like Mary Poppins, only you don't need the umbrella. Today is like that. Hold on a minute while I take a deep breath. . . .

"It worked! I floated across town and back. Actually I had to run an errand. For Mother. Someday I want to write a poem, 'Ode to the Supermarket.' All the women with their big fat selves stuffed into shifts and shorts, their hair up in huge pink and blue curlers so they'll look pretty for their husbands when they come home at night. Sort of touching when you think about it. And all the bright colored boxes screaming that they're the mostest, the best, and the produce counters. Ah, the produce counters! They should have an ode all to themselves. And everybody

117

moving in time to the music whether they know it or not. And the doors that open when you look at them. Magic.

"I tried to read Kafka like you told me to, but his colors are all gray and I don't dig his symbols. . . ."

Horace to July June 6th: (These letters aren't in sequence. I'm just picking them at random.)

". . . there's an undertone of wistfulness in your letters which I'm trying to fathom. And an air of secrecy about details as though unlike ordinary people you never eat or sleep or go to bed. But then of course you aren't ordinary people. Not in the least. Still I should like to be able to visualize you doing ordinary things and not always musing along with the muses or philossing with the philosophers. I remember you as quite earthy as well. Quite!"

I remember that I got up and went and looked in the mirror when I'd finished reading that one. I looked wistful. I also looked "earthy." Quite!

My reply to that was a long account of a day I spent at Holly Hill with Grandmother Greher canning tomatoes. *. . . July to Horace June 18th:*

". . . my grandmother is a very formal sort of person. Her invitation came by mail. . . ." I started to copy out the invitation for Horace to see because like all of her invitations it was quaint and charming and would give him a clearer picture of her than anything I might say. Reading it over I realized this was out of the question. There were too many references to the purpose of the undertaking, i.e., "I think every married woman should learn to preserve the harvest of the summer against the bleakness of winter." I wrote:

"She came to fetch me in her ten-year-old Lincoln at seven in the morning. 'We must pick them before the sun gets to them,' she said. I hadn't bargained on having to pick them myself since the tomato fields that lined the roads all the way to Holly Hill were alive with the Mexicans that come here every year at this time just for this purpose. My grandmother's acres were no exception. Men and women with babies packed on their backs, covered, though the temperature was in the 90's, from head to foot against the mosquitoes and the green stain the unripe tomatoes leave on their skin. I naturally thought we'd stop and pick up one of the full baskets from the side of the

118

road where the Mexicans put them to wait for the trucks from the packing house to pick them up but not my grandmother. 'It is impossible to tell the exact ripeness of the fruit unless you pick it yourself from the vine,' she said; 'the too ripe ones fall into your hand, the too green ones have to be twisted from the vine. The ones we want today are those that come with your hand when it leaves the vine.'

"Dressed like scarecrows we went out into the fields and began to pick. We weren't exactly working alongside the Mexicans because they pick green and we were picking red but they were near enough so that I could hear their Spanish talk and see how quickly they moved, filling ten baskets in the time it took me to do two. It made me feel quite humble and grateful too. I don't see how they stand living the way they do, always on the move and never knowing from one stop to the next whether they'll make enough to get by. I know that the farmers themselves are completely dependent on the weather and that when the Mexicans can't make enough the farmers can't either, but it's a lot easier to take a crop failure when you've got a roof over your head and the same good bed to sleep in every night even if, as my father pointed out, roof and bed are mortgaged to the hilt. My father sees everything from the bank's point of view. Whenever I get going on any subject like itinerate workers or the high cost of tenement living he tells Mother it's just a phase that I'll outgrow. I hope he's wrong.

"When Grandmother Greher and I had filled our baskets, we loaded them into the back seat of the Lincoln and chugged on up the hill to the house. Mathilda had breakfast waiting for us. My favorite. Corn bread, sausage, and grits. 'No hurry now,' Grandmother Greher said, 'they'll keep fine in the shade until we're ready.' Grandmother is tall and thin almost to the point of being skinny but she eats more than any of us.

" 'I don't know what she does with it,' Mother says.

" 'She burns it,' Father said, 'the way her Lincoln burns oil.'

"It took us most of the morning to peel the tomatoes even though the skin practically falls off after you dip them in boiling water. The rest is quite simple, and I

119

won't bore you with the details. Some of them we mashed through a strainer and some we cut in pieces and some we put up whole and I must say when it was all done and the jars, three dozen of them, were all topped and set out on the kitchen table to cool they looked with the sun shining on them like great overgrown rubies. I would never have believed that canning could be a truly creative experience. . . ."

Horace to July, June 26th:

". . . you were a doll to share your canning with me, and it did sort of help to make you real and not just some pixie dream I had and was trying not to wake from. I mean now that I can see you sweating it out in a tomato patch and stooped over pots and jars in somebody's kitchen it brings you closer. . . ."

I read this letter with a sense of discovery. I felt I had found there were areas in my life that still belonged so completely to myself that I might share them with someone other than Bo Jo without being in the least dishonest. What this sharing might be doing to Horace did not occur to me.

Bo Jo and I were just settling down to an even keel when the subject of my doctor came up. I naturally thought he'd be glad that I was going to have Dr. Pearless, whom everybody knows is tops, instead of Dr. Harvey, who is young and inexperienced. Instead, when I told him he hit the ceiling.

He said, "I'm fed up with your family running this whole show. Why the hell do they think I quit school and took a job if I didn't want to take the responsibility, be some sort of a man. What do they think I am? A gigolo hired for the duration?"

"They only want to help," I said. "That's all."

"Sure, sure, the best of everything for their little girl. Damnit *no!* This I'm doing, just this one thing. This I do. Who the hell's baby do they think it is? Theirs?"

For no special reason except that I was tired of our quarrels I began to cry, which I knew from experience would only make him madder, and it did.

"That's your answer for everything!" he said. "You *wring* my heart," he said, and started for the front door, which was *his* answer for everything. But with the door halfway open he stopped and slowly shut it again and came back into the room.

"I'm sorry I blew my stack," he said.

"I'm sorry I cried," I said.

"There ought to be some other way of deciding things between us," he said, sounding puzzled.

"Like talking about them," I said.

"You see," Bo Jo said, "this baby is beginning to mean something to me. It didn't at first. At first the only responsibility I felt was to you, what I owed to you, but now the baby begins to mean something. I begin to absorb the fact. I even find myself wondering sometimes if it will be a boy or a girl. And . . . and I want the responsibility for it, see? I actually *want* the responsibility."

"I think that's wonderful," I said. "I'm glad. I . . . I . . . just didn't realize. . . ."

"And I can't afford Dr. Pearless," Bo Jo said.

"I think I'll like Dr. Harvey better," I said, "because he's younger. And actually, who wants a private room? Nobody to talk to. . . ."

We looked at each other and grinned.

"I think this calls for a chocolate malted at the drugstore," Bo Jo said. "Go wash your face."

When we came home we went straight to bed. We talked awhile about the budget and about the baby and what we would name it. Jonathan, if it was a boy, and Allison, if it was a girl because we liked the names, and nobody's feelings could be hurt. And later when he made love to me it was different. Though he still didn't tell me that he loved me, I had the definite impression that for a little while he did. Very much.

The only doctor's office I was familiar with was Dr. Hapgood's, where Mother used to take us every year just before school opened for our annual checkup. His waiting room was big and musty and smelled of crayon wax almost as strongly as it smelled of the rubbing alcohol he used to clean the place where he was going to give us a shot. The boxes of crayons stood on the magazine rack along with various coloring books, and Grace and I forgot our fears by fighting over the least worn-down crayons and the prettiest coloring book until it was our turn to be

121

led into the inner sanctum where heaven knew what might await us. There were no crayons or coloring books in Dr. Harvey's waiting room, but I'm sure if there had been I would, out of habit and nervousness, have pounced on them. However, though there were three other women ahead of me I wasn't left idle for long. First, the nurse came and left me with a form to fill out with my birthdate, name and address, husband's occupation, number of previous pregnancies, et cetera. As soon as that was done, she whipped me into a tiny laboratory and took blood first from my arm and then from my finger and when that was done, handed me an empty glass jar as though it was some sort of reward for bravery like the candy mints Dr. Hapgood used to pass out after he'd given us a shot. I mumbled a bewildered "thank you" before I realized that I was being herded into the ladies' room and why.

Dr. Harvey was chubby, cheerful, and matter of fact. He said everything seemed in order. He asked me if I'd felt the baby move yet. I asked him how that felt.

"Like butterfly wings at first," he said. "Later you won't need to ask."

He gave me a list of things to eat every day and said he thought the baby would arrive around the fifteenth of October. The way he talked about the baby this and the baby that, as though it already had an existence, gave me a marvelous feeling of reality about everything.

When I walked back through the waiting room, there were several new patients waiting and one of them was balancing a baby across her knees. Its head lolloped like the neck was made of rubber. It couldn't have been more than a few weeks old, so I stopped to look at it. Gory was the last tiny baby I'd seen, or really looked at you might say, and that was so long ago I'd forgotten. This baby's eyes were open, but they kind of rolled around not seeing anything. Its mother was watching me with this smug expectant smile on her face waiting for me to tell her how beautiful it was. I tried to feel something toward it that wasn't revulsion and couldn't. Suddenly my legs felt all shaky and I was afraid if I didn't get out of there I'd faint.

"What a lot of hair it has," I said in a rush and made a beeline for the door.

Outside, the day was balmy and light. I steadied myself

against the iron railing that ran down the few steps to the street and took a couple of deep breaths. It was while I was standing there that I felt it ... the butterfly wings fluttering against the inner wall of me ... just as the doctor had described it. I held my breath and waited a moment and it happened again. Life. I was carrying a life. A gift. A trust. Forgotten entirely was that other baby that had failed to move me. This one was mine and quite beautiful I was sure.

I wanted to tell someone about it. Someone that didn't already know. I wanted to tell someone to whom it would be news. I thought of Lou.

She was wearing leotards and one of her husband's shirts judging by the size, and her eyes were red and swollen as though she'd been crying.

"I'm practicing," she said in a not very glad to see me voice, but she stepped back and held the door open, and I couldn't very well back out at that point.

There was some slow sweet music cooking on the stereo and nearby the stereo stood a tall metal tube that might at one time have been a floor lamp.

"The mike," Lou explained, looking a little embarrassed. "I can't practice without feeling like it's for real. I cozy up to that and shut my eyes and I'm gone."

"Don't let me interrupt," I said. "I'd honestly love to hear you sing."

"You don't know what you're saying!" But she looked pleased. "I was working out with 'Love in the Morning.' Want that?"

I sat down and she turned the stereo down, and grinning, made a megaphone with her hands cupped around her mouth. "Louella Consuela, the girl with the languid larynx will now lilt 'Love in the Morning.'" The grin, the tear-swollen eyes, gave her a clownish air. She turned the stereo up again and lovingly clutched the skeleton lamp and closed her eyes. When the music had spun around to where she wanted it, she tilted her head back and a little to one side and sang:

"Love in the morning
    Is the best kind of love
    The real test kind of love. . . ."

Her voice was low and true and surprisingly warm. I too shut my eyes and imagined the clink of waiters removing glasses, the hot perfumed smell of the women, the cloud of cigarette smoke drifting overhead.

"Without any warning
   It was love in the morning."

Her voice throbbed to a rising sweetness, dropped to a whisper:

"Without any warning
   The best kind of love
   The real test kind of love . . ."

Suddenly she broke off and flung the skeleton lamp to the floor. My eyes flew open. Dazed, it took me a second to return to the room and to Lou, who suddenly behind fists clenched to her mouth was crying.

"But you're good," I said. "Really good. I had no idea—"

"That son of a bitch! That damned son of a bitch," she cried.

I thought I must have missed a cue, that this must be a part of the song. I waited, mouth open, for the punch line.

"I could kill him," she said, "with my bare hands," she said, and unclenched her fists and held them out in front of her, rigid, like claws.

Still confused, I ventured a hoarse "Who?"

"Nick, that's who. My husband."

"Your husband?"

"Don't sound so shocked. Don't sound so ultra ultra." She glared at me. "I'll call him anything I want. True of false. Whatever I want. Today I am calling him a son of a bitch. Any objections?"

I shook my head.

"He has tricked me! He has trapped me! He has saddled me with a brat. I'm pregnant is what I am. And he agreed . . . he promised not to . . . Good-bye dreams! Hello slavery! Me, Lou Consuela, cornered, finished, at age eighteen." She flopped down in a chair, ankle on

124

knee, and bit at a stray wisp of hair. "You think I'm inhuman, hunh? A freak?"

I shook my head again.

"Look. I grew up in a house full of brats. All sizes. A new one every year. I was the oldest. The fall guy. I've put in my time. And over. In spite of the exposure I never learned to like the little snot-nosed, wet-seated varmints. You might even say I have an allergy. You might say I should never have got married. But then I forget. You've never met Nick. If Nick wants a girl to go to bed with him she goes. If he wants her to marry up with him she marries. You don't say no to Nick. But I'm saying no to his brat. No! No! No! You don't know a doctor, by any chance, do you? The right kind of doctor?"

"No," I said.

"There must be a way!" She got up and started walking around the room, taking big strides, angrily tossing her hair back from her face. I decided this was definitely not the day to tell her about October the fifteenth.

"How does Nick feel about it?" I said.

"I haven't told him. I'm hoping I won't have to. But I know how he'd feel all right. He's nuts about kids. A man can afford to be. What do they know about it?"

"When is the baby due?" I hoped she wouldn't say October. I felt like it would be bad luck if she did.

"Nine months from a certain picnic at Archers' Creek, that's when. It wasn't my idea, I can tell you! Making love on a raft out in the middle of a creek fifteen miles from home. But like I said, Nick is not a man you say no to."

"Maybe after a while it won't seem so bad. I mean if *he* wants it and you're crazy about him—"

"He is a yellow-bellied sloth, a rat-tailed hyena, and you are an absolute infant. What has being crazy about a man got to do with it? And just how crazy about me is he going to be when I start swelling up like a balloon? Him with his big weakness for flat-bellied women. What happens then, I ask you?"

"I don't know," I said, "but I think you ought to at least find out."

"I'm going to probably have to," Lou said, and fell to biting her nails.

It was all very depressing, and certainly took the edge off the way I'd felt when I first left Dr. Harvey's office.

When I got home I met Mother coming down the garage apartment steps.

"I thought your appointment was for ten," she said. "I've been waiting here since eleven and now I've simply got to get home for lunch."

"Why don't you stay and have lunch with me?" I said. I was no longer in any mood to talk about the baby, but I didn't want to be alone with my thoughts either.

My mother only hesitated a moment, weighing all the pros and cons, but something in my face must have decided her for she said, "Of course. But I'll have to run over the Hatty's and telephone. Your father hates mysteries."

While she was gone, I made iced tea and tuna fish sandwiches. Mary Ann had given me a pretty blue eyelet luncheon set which I'd not taken out of the box. I got that out and moved the jonquils and iris I'd picked in Hatty Barnes' garden that morning from the living room coffee table to the dining table.

"How pretty," Mother said. "Sorry to be so long. But you know Hatty. I had to hear all about the trip she's planning to take next fall ... the Himalayas no less. I wonder why. ... Now, dear, tell me about yourself. What did Dr. Harvey say?"

I told her what Dr. Harvey said, but all the while I was talking I was thinking of Lou and the crazy imbalance of things and when I'd finished Mother said, "Are you telling me everything? You seem depressed."

"Everything," I assured her. "It would seem I'm the picture of health. He didn't even seem to think I needed to lose weight."

"Well, that's something to be thankful for," my mother said. "Now if we could just work out some way for you to keep up with your schoolwork. ..."

"One thing at a time please," I said irritably. She frowned over the top of her iced-tea glass.

"I wish you and Bo Jo could get out more. See people. What do you do for fun?"

"We go to the movies," I said, "and lots of times Charlie Saunders drops by and some of the others. ..."

126

"We are having the Whites for dinner midday Sunday. They aren't young, but at least they're a lot younger than your father and I. Why don't you and Bo Jo join us? I think you might like them. I know you'll like her. They're from Washington . . . the state . . . he's here in some sort of advisory capacity with the new textile plant and she's much interested in starting a little theatre. Seems she directed the children's theatre in . . . in . . . whatever the town was where they lived. . . ."

"I would love to meet her," I said. "I'll ask Bo Jo."

"Why? Do you have something else planned?"

"No. I just better ask him, that's all."

"Whatever you wish. However, you'll soon learn it's the woman who arranges the social life. . . . I made the plans and then tell your father about them. He's usually pleased but if I asked him in advance we'd never go anywhere."

"Bo Jo likes it better when I ask," I said.

"In that case . . ." Mother shrugged. "We'll eat about one."

I knew that they always ate about one on Sunday. I also knew that when they had guests or even sometimes when they didn't they had a cocktail or a highball or even just a glass of sherry beforehand, which they served at about twelve thirty. If she hadn't specified any particular time for lunch, knowing that I knew the time, I probably wouldn't have given it a thought, but as it was I did.

I said, "What time are the Whites coming?"

"Noonish," she said, "but you'd probably get awfully bored sitting around watching us drink cocktails."

"Oh, Mother!" I said. "When are you going to stop thinking of us as children?"

"When you no longer are," Mother said matter-of-factly and swooped up the dishes and glasses and put them in the sink.

"I'll do that," I said, and took the dishrag out of her hand.

"Then I'll dry," Mother said.

"I don't dry. I just let them drain."

"Oh," Mother said, "how very clever of you." She meant it. Like I'd invented something. "Then if I can't be of any help I'll be running along. The lunch was good, just right. . . ."

"I didn't really *do* anything."

"I think you do too much as it is. . . . Hatty Barnes was telling me you even iron your own sheets as well as Bo Jo's shirts."

"How snoopy of her! What else did she tell you?"

"That you quarrel a lot," Mother said, and looked at me, frowning again. "I suppose it's to be expected, but I wish . . ."

Her voice trailed off and I said, "Oh, for heaven's sake. All young married people quarrel."

Mother gave me a quizzical sad little look and began stuffing handkerchief and gloves into her pocketbook. At the door she turned and said in that overly casual way I'd learned long ago meant she was about to give voice to something she'd been turning over in her mind for days, "And do, darling, have a wifely word with Bo Jo about his table manners. I'm sure it's just a matter of his not thinking."

She and I both knew it was no such thing. It was a matter of his not knowing. Though I had already given some thought as to how I could bring up the subject without hurting his feelings, having the suggestion come from Mother made me furious. By the time I caught my breath she was gone. I stood staring at the door that had closed behind her, thinking of all the things I should have said. . . . That there were a lot of things more important in a man's character than his table manners. . . . That their precious Gory could bear some watching in this area. . . . That Bo Jo's table manners were actually none of their business. I had never felt so loyal toward Bo Jo as I did at that moment. Nor so protective. It hurt me that my parents so obviously neither liked nor approved of him. Their opinion had always meant a lot to me. So much so that if I made a friend and found they didn't like her I could never have quite the same feeling for her. Of course, I'd known they hadn't really gone for Bo Jo from the beginning, but my feelings toward him were so strong that it didn't matter. But once I was married to him it did matter. I don't think Bo Jo realized what a nonentity he was as far as they were concerned or he wouldn't have tried as hard to please them as he did, but I was always
128

afraid he might find out, which made me nervous whenever we were all together.

When Bo Jo came in that evening, I hugged him extra hard and treated him to his special favorite supper ... hamburgers, French fries, and chocolate ice cream. But the worst of it was that the very next time I got mad with him I heard myself shouting at him that the least he could do was pick up his fork when he ate and keep his arms off the table, though the subject had absolutely nothing to do with what we were fighting about. It stopped him dead in his tracks. He looked as though I'd pulled a knife right out of thin air and plunged it into him. I immediately said that I didn't mean it, that I was sorry, but he drew back, his eyes clouded and hurt.

"Uncouth is the word," he said, and when I tried to touch him, to console him, he pushed my hand away. It was time for him to go to work and he went. I had a good cry after he left. He was all right that night or pretending to be. Neither of us ever mentioned that ghastly moment of truth again. He passed the Sunday dinner with the Whites with flying colors, but I took no pleasure in the fact. I didn't think Mr. White held a candle to Bo Jo in looks and she was one of these intellectually charged people that couldn't talk about anything but herself ... what *she* read, what *she* thought. Meeting them gave me something to write to Horace about, but aside from that it was a waste. Which was too bad since actually I was beginning to be a little desperate about our social life which was practically nonexistent. Charlie Saunders was constantly underfoot but he had stopped bringing Alicia Helms with him which at first made me very happy until I found that it just meant that Charlie and Bo Jo paired off and left me out of it. They'd sit up and watch whole baseball games by the hour without so much as a word to me. Though that was less lonesome making than when they went charging off together to play pool and drink beer until all hours.

I made an attempt to improve the situation. Mary Ann's Alan came for a weekend and we asked the two of them around for coffee and dessert one night after supper. I wanted to ask them for supper but we couldn't afford a steak or anything really good in the meat line and I didn't

129

feel sure enough of myself in the casserole area. Bo Jo's mother made a devil's food cake and my mother brought us four parfait glasses and spoons, which added some class to what would have otherwise been just a plain chocolate sundae.

I'd heard enough about Alan to fill a book, but I had never met him before. I didn't really expect him to be all the things Mary Ann had said he was. When someone's in love you take what they say about HIM and divide it by two and subtract. But Alan was just about as she'd pictured—tall and quiet and smooth-looking with a soft voice and an accent that shounded like Eastern boarding schools and a year abroad at some time in his life.

I guess Mary Ann had told him about Bo Jo's football record because he started right in talking football with him. She also must have dredged up those long-ago plays in Grandmother Greher's carriage house because he said he knew I was interested in the theatre. He was dear and charming and I was very happy for Mary Ann, but it was more as though he was entertaining us, trying to make us relaxed and comfortable in a strange place, than vice versa, and I was afraid when they were married Mary Ann and I would find ourselves even farther apart than ever in spite of the fact that he and Bo Jo got along like a house afire. Or seemed to.

"Now there's a real gent," Bo Jo said after they left.

"Yes," I said, "and just right for Mary Ann. Did you notice how he hardly took his eyes off her the whole time?"

Bo Jo grunted and I should have shut up then and there and gone to bed. Both of us were tired and it had been a strain getting ready for them. But there was a hurt knot forming in my chest and I pushed on.

"And the way he put his arm around her when they were leaving. As though she were the most beautiful and adored woman in the world."

"Well, as far as he's concerned she is," Bo Jo said, and kicked off his shoes and started toward the bedroom.

"I wonder what he thought about us."

"I think he liked us. I think he had a good time."

"I mean about us, 'we.' The togetherness bit."

Bo Jo grunted again and I said, "Why don't you ever

130

show me any affection in public? I was downright embarrassed tonight by your lack of affection. Most of the time I don't think you even remembered I was there."

"Aw, come off it, July. Come to bed and I'll show you some affection."

"You make it sound *so* romantic." I was emptying cups in the sink and I went right on emptying them. Bo Jo came up behind me and put his arms around my waist. This usually melted me, but the picture of Alan and Mary Ann was still too fresh in my mind. I stiffened and his arms fell away.

"What do you want? A dozen roses every time?" he said.

"Well, something to tell me how you feel about me."

"When I'm in bed with you I'm telling you. Sometimes I even think you hear me."

"I do. I do. Sometimes. Other times I think I could be just anybody."

"What do you mean by that crack?"

"It wasn't a crack. Sometimes I need a buildup. A few kind words."

"For Christ's sake! Words! You mean you need a blueprint of my emotions? I wouldn't be making love to you if I didn't want you."

"All boys want."

"Any girl? Any time? Is that what you think?"

"Well, don't they?"

"Hell, no!"

"Maybe not *any* girl but it isn't so necessary for them to be emotionally involved."

"Well, I am!"

"Emotionally involved?"

"Naturally. You're my wife, aren't you? You're going to have my baby. Why wouldn't I be?" He walked over to the coffee table, picked up a magazine, opened it, slammed it back down on the table, "Look, can't we go to bed? Just go to bed? I'm tired. I want you. Can't we just take it from there?"

"Sure," I said, "sure."

But when he got in bed beside me I found I was still feeling hurt and withdrawn. I guess I was still thinking about Mary Ann and Alan . . . feeling sorry for myself. I

131

just wasn't with it. I tried to pretend but Bo Jo wasn't fooled. He kissed me once and muttered a cross "good night" climbed into his own bed.

I woke up much later. The moon was almost full. It shone through Hatty Barnes' sleazie gauze curtains as though they weren't there. Bo Jo's bed was right under the window and I could see him quite clearly. He slept on his back, one arm crooked above his head, his closed and motionless face turned toward the moonlight. I got up and went over and looked at him, the square snubbed nose, the stubbly hair almost colorless in this light. He looked, I thought, terribly young and defenseless and sweet.

As I leaned above him the baby lurched inside me and for a moment the baby inside me and the youth on the bed seemed one and the same and I somehow responsible for them both.

I lay down beside Bo Jo and whispered to him that I was sorry. I'm not sure he heard the words, but something got through to him for slowly his eyes opened. He looked at me, dazed and guileless with sleep, and this time when he put his arms around me I was there. I was with it and he knew it.

A few weeks after my depressing talk with Lou, she came bouncing into the apartment looking like the cat that had swallowed the canary.

"It's all set," she said. "I've found someone in the business, and as luck would have it Nick has to go to New York tomorrow for a couple of days. I just wanted *someone* to know in case, well just in case . . ."

"In case you should just happen to die? Oh, Lou," I said, "you shouldn't, you really shouldn't. If you should ever be sorry, you would be sorry all the rest of your life. It could be a terrible burden."

"That's not the kind of burden I'm worried about right now." She actually smiled.

"And it's very dangerous, you know."

"This man is tops in the field. I've made inquires . ."

"Then he probably costs a fortune," I said. "And where will you get the money?"

"I've already got it," she said. "I borrowed it. From a loan company. Fifty percent interest. But they don't ask any questions."

"That's illegal," I said. I wasn't a banker's daughter for nothing.

"That's their problem," Lou said. "I got my own Namey paying them back without Nick knowing. And so starting next week between the hours of nine and five you may find me behind the stocking counter at Plenty's. I shall tell Nick I am bored and lonely and wish to make a study of humanity. He won't like it, but after I cry a little while he'll give in."

"Where is this place?" I said.

"Plenty's."

"No, this place you're going tomorrow."

"I am not allowed to divulge. As a matter of fact, I am not 'allowed' to tell another living soul anything about it at all."

"You have to go all alone?"

"Gruesome, isn't it? But I'll be so elated when it's over none of the rest will matter."

"Tomorrow you said?"

"Tomorrow at ten A.M. to be exact."

"And when do you get home? I mean I think somebody ought to be there when you get home."

"It all depends. Without complications he said by late afternoon or early evening. Frankly I would most certainly appreciate it if you were there. Not that it's necessary, but I would most certainly appreciate it."

"I wish you'd change your mind. Would it make any difference if you knew I was going to have a baby too? That we're both in the same boat?"

"You mean we walk woman's noble path to motherhood together? No, thanks. And no lectures please. I mean I'm real happy for you if that's what you want. But leave me out of it."

Lou left a key to their house with me in case she shouldn't have got back before I got there. I didn't say anything to Bo Jo about any of this. He hadn't liked Lou in the beginning, and I didn't think this present situation would improve anything. But I didn't want him to worry or grown hungry so I cooked a casserole and left it on top of the stove with a note. I didn't want to tell him where I was going, so I just said I might be late. He would undoubtedly think I was at Mother's.

133

I got to Lou's bungalow at about five. The door was open and the screen door was unlatched, so I walked in and called from the living room. There wasn't any answer so I went on back to the bedroom. The shades were drawn. Lou lay on the bed so still that at first I thought she slept, but in a moment she turned her head and looked at me. I say looked at me—actually she fixed on me the eyes of a wounded animal, wide and fearful and still. Nor was there any look of recognition in them.

"Are you all right?" I said.

"Yes." Her voice was a whisper. Her lips looked dry.

"I'll get you some water." I went out to the kitchen and got out ice and put it in a glass and poured the water over it. When I came back she lifted her head a little, and I held the glass to her mouth. I still was hardly sure she knew me.

"Are you sure you're all right?" I said, and pulled a chair up to the bed and sat down.

"Quite sure. He told me what to look for." I was relieved to hear her speak out.

"Are you in much pain?"

"Some. But he gave me pills to take if . . ."

"I planned to fix you some supper," I said, "but I guess you don't want any."

She shook her head.

"Not even some soup?"

She shook her head again and suddenly out of those sick animal eyes tears sprouted. "It was terrible," she said. "It was a degradation."

I tried to think of something comforting to say, but I hadn't come prepared to comfort her. I hadn't thought she'd need it. I could think of nothing. Pretty soon her tears stopped and she closed her eyes. Her face was white and drawn and the long hair lanked around it damp and lifeless. It was hard to believe that she had ever been pretty and happy. I felt like crying myself.

I thought that she was asleep but in a little while, her eyes still closed, she said, "It was all wrong. I shouldn't have done it."

I took her hand and squeezed it. It was all I could think of to do. We sat that way I don't know how long.

134

She finally opened her eyes and said, "It must be very late. Bo Jo will be wondering where you are."

"I thought perhaps I might call Hatty Barnes and ask her to have him call me. I don't think you ought to be alone tonight."

"I'm all right. Everything went like a breeze they said. I'll just take one of those pills they gave me and float away."

"I still think . . ."

"Don't. I'll call you if I need you."

"But we don't have a phone."

"Then I'll call your friend Hatty whatever her name is."

"Promise?"

"If it'll make you feel better. July?"

I turned at the door. Waited.

"Did you want this baby you're having?"

It wasn't a fair question. Not at this time, in this place.

"I want it now," I said. "I very much want it now."

"But you didn't at first."

"Things change," I said.

"Thanks for nothing," she said.

"I'm sorry," I said, and I was, but she shouldn't have asked.

Outside it was dark and it was a good ten blocks to our apartment, but I wanted to walk. I felt I needed the fresh air.

From a half a block away I could hear Bo Jo practicing on the trombone. Up and down the scale and down and up. It was bad enough with the windows and doors shut, but now in summer with them open I wondered how long it would be before the neighbors complained. I ran up the steps knowing the sooner I got there the sooner the noise would stop, but he just looked at me and went right on.

Charlie Saunders was sprawled on the couch wearing his Arcadia usher's outfit. I couldn't tell from the look of him if he were on his way to work or on his way home. I fervently hoped it was the former because then at least there'd be some sort of deadline. Neither of them gave me more than a cursory greeting, and I had the definite feeling that they'd been talking about me and had reached

135

some sort of mutual conclusion involving how I was to be treated on my return.

The note I'd left Bo Jo and the casserole were still on the dining table, and neither looked as though it had been touched. For some reason I found the scene wildly irritating. It was the first time he'd come home to find me gone and I suppose I'd hoped he would have missed me, that he would give me the same big welcome I gave him every evening when he got home.

"I bet you've been boozing," he finally said. "You and that Consuela girl."

"How did you know where I was?" I said, too surprised to dissemble.

"Because I called everywhere else. So than it figured."

"I'm seeing flying saucers," Charlie Saunders said, coming into the kitchen area.

"O.K., so that's where I was. *You* can have friends." I gave a passing glance in Charlie's direction. "So can I."

"Not the kind of friends that send you home stewed to the gills."

"Oh? So?" Another meaningful glance at Charlie.

"What makes you think she's stewed?" Charlie said.

"She's never acted like this before. I've never seen her like this before."

"There's always a first time," Charlie said. "Women don't have to be stewed to act crazy. Sometimes all you gotta do is look at them wrong."

"Let me smell your breath," Bo Jo said, walking up close to me. I grabbed a pot.

"Get out of here!" I said. "Both of you! I don't care if I never see you again. And that goes for Charlie too. E-SPEC-IALLY Charlie!"

Of course, as soon as they, looking hurt and repentant, took themselves off, I began to cry.

I didn't cry long. I went and sat down on the couch and wondered how I'd explain myself to Bo Jo. Wondered if there was anything to say except that I was sorry. His coat was hanging over a chair, and I saw there was a long white envelope sticking out of the outside pocket. I went to hang the coat up and couldn't help noticing the return address on the envelope. I mean it was staring me right in the face ... "Coach Bauman" at the State University. I

136

have little or no respect for the kind of people who read other people's mail, but the temptation was too much. The envelope had been torn open at one end and I took the letter out and read it, and then I put it back in the envelope and put the envelope back in the coat pocket and hung the coat up in the closet.

Evidently nobody had told Coach Bauman that Bo Jo had dropped out of school. The letter said, "Hope you are making up the courses you were required to make up, this summer. We are starting practice in mid-August and look forward to seeing you then."

No wonder Bo Jo had been upset! I waited up until he came home. I hoped he would be sober so we could talk, and he was. He didn't even smell of beer. He smelled faintly of perfume and there was a small lipstick mark behind his ear. Alicia Helms, no doubt, giving out with the understanding. It took every ounce of will power I had not to mention it. When I said I had something I wanted to talk to him about he turned beet red and stuck out his chin as if he were ready for the punch.

"I saw that letter from Coach Bauman," I said. "As a matter of fact, I read it."

He was so relieved that that was what I wanted to talk to him about that he forgot to be mad because I'd snooped through his mail.

"Oh, that. . . ." He spread his hands in a "so what" gesture.

"It must have made you feel terrible," I said. "I know it made me."

"We've been through all that," he said. "Why feel terrible?"

"It occurred to me that maybe after the baby, after we have the baby, something could be worked out."

"Like what?"

"Like you going back to school for a few months and then to the University."

"What kind of dream world is that? *After* we have the baby is when I really have to put my nose to the grindstone."

"The baby and I could live with Mother and Father awhile. I could take a secretarial course or something. . . ."

"I can't think that far ahead," Bo Jo said. "Actually I can't think any further ahead than tomorrow and after that the next day." He leaned over and propped his head in his hands. "Or is it that you want out? Is that what you want?"

Until that moment I'd honestly been thinking only in terms of him, of how the letter must have upset him. "Of course not," I said. But for a minute a door opened in my head and through it I saw myself gay and carefree again, going to house parties at Bowers with Alan's friend from South America, and going to Princeton weekends with Horace. Before the door closed again, I even saw myself in a wedding dress walking up a flower-strewn aisle to meet some nameless bridegroom who would be waiting there with adoration in his eyes.

I shook my head to shake it free. I said, "Of course not. What I want is to make a success of our marriage, a home for our baby."

"In that case," he said, "let's leave sleeping dogs sleep or however the saying goes. . . ." He got up and started for the bedroom.

I followed him in and sat down on the edge of my bed and watched Bo Jo undress. I'd gotten so I no longer felt self-conscious about watching him. I'd grown used to the way he looked without clothes. I admired the way his shoulders sloped forward a little from the back like the shoulders of a prizefighter going into the ring, and I thought the long firm muscles in his legs and calves were beautiful like the line drawings one sees in anatomy books.

"I guess I better tell you why I went to Lou's this afternoon . . . why I was late getting home."

"It's not that important. Like you said, I guess if I can have my friends you're entitled to yours."

"Lou needs me," I said. "At least she did this afternoon. That's why I went over there. The only reason."

"Where was her husband?"

"He had to go to New York."

"Why couldn't you have told me . . . in the note you left? When I first saw that note sitting on top of the casserole supper some crazy ideas went through my head. I was almost scared to read it with Charlie watching me.

138

And then when I did read it, I didn't know any more than I did to start with."

"I couldn't tell you the whole thing in a note. I actually didn't plan to tell you anything at all, but I want you to know I'm not the kind of person you accused me of being."

"Lou is."

"Not really. I've never seen her drink anything but Cokes. She was sick and by herself. That's why I went over."

"If Charlie hadn't come home with me I probably wouldn't have thought much about it. Charlie thinks you're great. A great little wife."

"He does?" I honestly found this hard to believe.

"Yeah," Bo Jo said, and got into bed, "because that's what I tell him." He pulled the blanket up to his eyes and then crossed his eyes at me, a thing he does to make me laugh when he has said something nice that he's afraid I'm going to make a big hearts-and-flowers thing about.

I undressed in the bathroom because I was beginning to be self-conscious about the various shapes my body was taking on and when I came back Bo Jo had turned off the light. I thought he was asleep but in a few minutes he said, "What was the matter with Lou?"

"She had an abortion." It was easier to say with the lights out.

"You mean a miscarriage?"

"No. She didn't want the baby."

"Nick too?"

"He didn't know. Doesn't know."

Bo Jo was silent for so long I again thought he slept but just as I myself was about to drop off he said, "I guess you know I might have gone along with something like that in the beginning."

"I know."

"But no more," Bo Jo said. "Absolutely not. I am glad you never even considered it."

"I think Lou is already sorry."

"What was eating her? She got a boy friend or something on the side?"

"She just doesn't want kids. She doesn't like them. She

139

had too many little brothers and sisters to take care of when she was little."

"Does Nick want kids?"

"Yes, she says he does."

"God help her then if he ever finds out. If he ever finds out, he'll kill her."

My first waking feeling was one of absolute depression, and it had nothing to do with Bo Jo and me. I had to wake up a little before I realized it had to do with Lou. Lou, all alone and sick. I determined to go over there the minute Bo Jo left the house, but just as I was about to leave, Hatty Barnes called to me from the garden that someone wanted me on the telephone. It was Lou.

She said, "I just wanted you to know I'm all right." She sounded fine.

"Also," she said, "forget the sackcloth and ashes bit. That was just something brought on by the pills. Actually I feel like I just escaped from Sing Sing. I feel wonderful."

"I was about to come over," I said.

"No need. But thanks for the visiting nurse act anyway. I'll be seeing you. . . ."

I had thought that when school let out, Bo Jo and I would have more social life. I'd even dreamed of the old gang dropping around for evenings of guitar playing and singing and talk about books and politics and how we'd change the world if we had the chance. I'd even looked up some inexpensive recipes in the cookbook Gory gave me just in case. But it didn't work out that way. Mary Ann took off the day after school closed to visit Alan's family in Pittsburgh. Tommy Ryan was counseloring at a camp, Charlie Saunders was going to summer school, for which I should have been thankful but somehow wasn't. So, except for the letters from Horace Clark, which came every week and grew longer and longer, I had practically no social life at all.

Bo Jo said the answer was to make some new friends, and one night he invited a couple of the clerks from the bank and their wives over for coffee and dessert. I think Bo Jo enjoyed it. He and the men talked sports and shop, but I couldn't find anything to talk to the women about so we just listened to the men, and when one of the couples

140

invited us to their house I found I just couldn't face another evening like that one. I told Bo Jo I had a headache.

I couldn't help thinking it was too bad that Bo Jo had taken such a dislike to Lou and that Lou's husband was so much older than we were. At least they would have been fun. However, as it turned out maybe it's just as well we didn't get involved with them. One late afternoon I was trying to drown some hiccoughs in a glass of water drunk from the wrong side of the glass when Lou walked in. She was dressed for the city in a black gabardine skirt, white nylon blouse, and black patent leather pumps with teeter-totter heels, and she was carrying a suitcase. There were dark circles under her eyes, and there was a black- and blue-mark the size of a quarter on her cheek. I hadn't seen her in weeks, since she started working at Plenty's to be exact, and I was shocked at how thin she'd got.

She said, "What on earth are you doing with that glass? Trying to fall into it?"

"Hiccoughs," I said.

"A paper bag is better," Lou said. "You breathe into it."

"What are you doing with that suitcase?" I said.

"Trying to catch a bus," she said, "but the damned thing is an hour late."

"Taking a vacation?"

"You might call it that. New scenery. New faces . . ." Her voice trailed off, and she sat down and lit a cigarette and smoothed the black skirt over her knees.

"Chicago?" I said.

"I haven't decided yet. I haven't decided whether to try New York while I've got the money to get there or go back to the old briar patch."

"What does Nick—"

"He doesn't!" she said. "As a matter of fact, he doesn't know I'm going anywhere." She glanced at her watch. "Not yet. And when he does find out he'll probably come tearing over here looking for me. He knows you're about the only friend I've got in this snake-bellied village. So maybe I shouldn't have come here, but he won't be home until six thirty, and after that it'll take him a while to

141

register to the fact that his everloving has taken a walkout powder."

"Oh, Lou! You don't really mean it!"

"He found out about the operation," she said, and put her cigarette out and lit another. "I got behind in my payments to the loan company so they got one of their henchmen to pay us a visit. And so . . ." she finished, as though that were explanation enough.

"And so?" I prodded.

"Nick called me a murderess. He said I'd cheated him. He said I'd cheated God. I didn't think he believed in God. I still don't. I think he invented Him to punish me. He said he was going to kill me."

"That bruise on your face," I said, "did he . . ."

Her fingers moved to the spot on her cheek and incredibly her face softened. "Yes," she said, "that's his mark. But," and her lips trembled, "that was over two weeks ago, and he hasn't touched me since. Not once."

"So why leave now?" I said. "Just when things are looking up?"

"I said he hadn't touched me. Not in any way." Again she touched the spot on her cheek with that strange tenderness. "You can't go on living with a man who won't touch you."

"But I don't think you should leave him," I said. "He's hurt. He'll get over it."

"Sure, sure, if I get down on my knees . . . if I promise to make it up to him with another baby. Right away. Nine months and thirty minutes from now. Blackmail is what it is. His forgiveness for my freedom. Oh, no. Don't think I haven't thought about it." She got up and walked over to the stereo and turned it on. The record that happened to be on it was a Chopin sonata. She scowled, shrugged, left it on. "It would be fine for a while, and then I'd start thinking about how he'd trapped me into the deal; I'd start thinking about all the things I wanted to do and now couldn't, all because I had to go on my knees to him. The time to think about all that is now. Not after it's too late. Maybe this is a sign. An omen. A break."

"I thought you loved Nick," I said. "I thought you were crazy about him."

"Now you sound just like him. 'If you loved me how

142

could you kill my baby?' 'If you loved me you'd want to make it up to me.' What about if *he* loved *me*? What about *my* feelings on the subject?" She glared at me as though I were Nick himself. "What about the cold sickness in the pit of my stomach I get from just thinking about a baby!"

"Maybe you should see a marriage counselor," I said. "Maybe both of you should."

"A marriage counselor? Nick and me?" She started to laugh; she doubled over with laughter. "I have now heard everything," she said. "I have now heard everything under the sun!" She paused, gasping for breath. "Well, thanks for the light touch at the end. I always like a light touch at the end myself." She gathered up her pocketbook and suitcase, still erupting into little spasms of laughter. "Nick and me . . . a marriage counselor . . ."

I didn't think it was funny or understand why she should. I said somewhat coldly, "If Nick does come here looking for you what shall I tell him?"

"Tell him? There's nothing to tell him. Nothing that he doesn't already know."

I made one more try. "Does he know how sorry you were? Right after the operation? Does he know you wished you hadn't had it?"

"I don't remember that much about it," she said, her eyes sliding past me to the door. "Well, I'll write when I get settled. And you let me hear when the baby comes. When is it supposed to come, by the way?"

"October," I said. "October the fifteenth."

"I'll be thinking about you on that date," Lou said, "and counting my blessings."

Bo Jo and I were just finishing supper when Nick came looking for Lou. He stormed into the apartment without knocking as though he were sure he'd find Lou there and thought this gave him the right to crash the gate. I'd only seen his pictures hanging around their place, but I knew right off who he was. His were not the kind of looks you forget right away, coal-black hair, coal-black eyes, a big crooked nose with deep lines at either side, a parenthesis framing his mouth. Seeing us seated, so quiet a twosome, at our supper table, he halted just past the threshold, like some raging animal held at bay by his own doubt. Bo Jo, fork in air, swallowed his mouthful of peas and said, "What the hell!" And to me, "Who does he think he is?"

I hadn't told him yet about Lou's departure, and Nick didn't give me the chance to now.

"Where is she?" he said. "Where's my wife?"

"What the hell!" Bo Jo said again, and started to get up out of his chair, but I managed to kick him under the table.

"This is Nick," I said to Bo Jo, "Lou's husband. Nick, this is my husband, Bo Jo."

Nick's head jerked in some sort of acknowledgment of the introduction, and Bo Jo said, "Whyn't you say so? Sit down. July'll get you some coffee."

"I haven't got time for coffee," Nick said. "I'm looking for my wife." As he spoke, his eyes raked the apartment. Not satisfied with this he went and looked through the open bedroom door. In the few seconds that his back was turned I tried to convey to Bo Jo with a silent moving of my lips that Lou had run away.

He must have got my message. His look of confused annoyance faded and he said, "You'll not find her in there, old boy."

Nick whirled on me then. *"You* know where she is! I could read that the minute I walked in."

"Yes," I said, noting with relief that the clock over the stove said six-forty-five, "I do know that she's left town. But I don't know where she went. She took a bus."

"Left town? Walked out on me?" The anger drained out of his face, leaving it pale and uncertain.

"She said she left you a note."

"Sure. Sure. She left a note. But what the hell does that mean? She's threatened to leave before. All it meant before was 'come and get me.'"

"Maybe that's what it meant this time," Bo Jo said, and got up and poured an extra cup of coffee and put it down at the empty place at the table. "If I had a drink in the house . . . but I haven't. How about trying this for size?"

I wished he hadn't done this. I didn't think Lou had meant "come and get me" this time, and Nick scared me. First his rage and now, his pain.

There was a man, when I was a little girl, who had a fruit stand on River Street. He was surly and dark and
144

vibrating with life. I was reminded of him now. I had been both fascinated and repelled by him and always managed to find something in a store window farther down the street to absorb my attention while my mother made her purchases. I was surprised to hear one day that he had died, an ordinary death, just like other men, in his bed, in his sleep. I had expected more from him than that.

Uneasily I watched Nick take the proffered seat at the table, swig down the coffee and hold out the cup for a refill.

"I should be glad," he said. "I should be glad to get rid of her. Every day I run into dames with more class, more style. Dames just asking for it. . . ." He scowled at the far wall for a moment and then turned his eyes on me, on my protruding maternity dress. "You were her friend. The only one she had here. Why couldn't you have stopped her?"

I shook my head, "She had her suitcase with her. She was on her way to the bus."

"Hell, I don't mean today. I mean the other thing. The baby?"

Again I shook my head, but I didn't say anything. Anything I said could only make it worse for him.

"If she had just told me I could have talked her out of it. Made her see. She's just a kid. With a lot of ideas. Big ideas. I could have talked her out of it," he repeated. "Where does that bus go from here?" he said. "The one she took. . . ."

"Just to Savannah," I said. "From there you can get a bus to most anywhere."

"New York, most likely." He spoke more to himself than to us. "She'd be too proud to go back to Chicago to her folks. Never got along with them anyway. New York. Her and her crazy dreams. She'll starve to death in a month." He got up. "Thanks for the coffee."

"Think nothing of it," said Bo Jo.

"Are you going after her?" I said.

"What the hell else?"

When he'd gone Bo Jo said, "He's nuts. That girl's no good."

"He loves her," I said. "It's as simple as that."

"Nothing is as simple as that," Bo Jo said.

Bo Jo was right. A few weeks later I came across an ad in the help wanted section of the Trilby *Times*. Braithwaite Farms was advertising for a new horse trainer. It could mean anything or nothing, but certainly meant that even if Nick had found Lou and they had had a reconciliation they would not be returning to Trilby. I was consumed with curiosity. I even called the Farms one day and asked to speak to Mr. Consuela, only to be told that he had resigned and that they didn't know where he'd gone.

I had all but stopped wondering about them when a letter came from Lou. It was postmarked New York and written on hotel stationery. Her handwriting was elaborately curlicued and uncertainly punctuated and though it wasn't terribly long it took awhile to read.

DEAR JULY,

I haven't written before because I honestly and truly haven't had a minutes since I landed in this fabulous town. It is everything and more than I ever expected! Something doing every minute. At first it was tough going and I made a lot of mistakes, like taking a room at the Y.W.C.A. and dressing like I was on my way out to a ball when I went job hunting and getting mixed up with an agent who took about every cent I had (he called it a "maintenance" fee) just to get me interviews with the managers of a bunch of cheap joints. I was forced to take a job as a waitress in one of them which actually turned out to be the best thing that could have happened on account of one of the regulars, a funny little crippled guy who came in every night about nine with the same woman (turns out he's married and this is the place where he meets his girl friend so as to be sure he doesn't run into anybody he knows). His tips were so small nobody wanted to wait on him so, I being new, took on the job. I was the first one that didn't give him the cold look or switch my backside in an insulting way when he'd dish out the nightly quarter. For that he and his girl friend took a liking to me and got so they'd ask me questions about myself. Turns out his nephew owns a chain of bistros. Turns out they're looking for a singer. Somebody new, willing to start small and take out some of her pay in free chow. I auditioned and got the job. The place was small and the address not too hot but I can't tell you the thrill I got that first night standing up in front of the mike with a live audience and the spotlight running up and down me like sunshine and knowing that outside was New York.

I hadn't been there a month before a talent scout from the Purple Plum spotted me one night and told me if I'd take a couple of lessons and then come see them they might have something for me. I went back to the waitress job part-time so's to pay for the lessons and got the job at the Purple Plum where I still am. I go on three times a night. Who knows maybe sometime you can tell people you knew me when!?!

In case you think I snitched this fancy hotel stationery I didn't. I actually live here! There's a guy who's paying for it. He is married but all of the most eligible men in New York are. He is tall and has a very distinguished prematurely gray hair and drives a Corvair. He also is very nice.

Well, I guess this just about covers everything and proves that everything works out for the best. Please write.

Love,
Lou.

P.S. Nick came up here looking for me. An erstwhile friend of mine at the Y told him where I was. It was while I was still waitressing and I don't mind admitting I was glad to see him. He wanted me to come back. He even said he would get a job in one of the stables in this area. That night I told him, I don't mind admitting, that I would. But in the morning I came to my senses. I don't know where he is now. I miss him sometimes but you can't have everything.

L.

I didn't show this letter to Bo Jo. And I didn't answer it. I didn't know what to say. I never heard from Lou again. Or anything about her. But a year or so after that a bunch of us were watching the Belmont races on TV and

I caught a glimpse of Nick. It seems he had trained the runner-up and they showed him shaking hands with its owner. He looked as handsome as ever.

As I grew daily more pregnant, my letters to Horace became more and more difficult to write. I honestly don't know why I kept on with them. The necessity to communicate with someone like Horace was fading fast as Bo Jo and I found more to talk about. Bo Jo and I may not have had much in common to start with . . . actually nothing except school and the group we ran around with—and the minute we got married there wasn't even that—but living with a person over a period of time is about the most "in common" thing you can have with anyone I was beginning to find. We still looked at television more than was good for us but we had got in the habit of sitting down for a cup of coffee when he got home from work to talk over the day's happenings. He still hated his job at the bank but spilling his grievances to me at the end of the day took some of the pressure off and he seemed honestly interested in my small encounters with the meat man at the supermarket, with Hatty Barnes over the light bill, with the sweater I was trying to knit for the baby. We talked a lot about the baby. In his spare time Bo Jo was making a cradle in his father's workshop. He said it was to save money on a crib, but he refused to use anything but the best of everything and by the time it was done we could have bought a crib at half the price. His father was cruel enough to point this out, a thing I wouldn't have done for the world. I was afraid Bo Jo would be furious or hurt, but he didn't bat an eye. I realized then that saving money had never been the point.

When we were alone together we were all right. Most of the time, anyhow. It was only around my family or his that we grew uncomfortable with each other and sometimes ended up when we got home fighting over some completely unrelated subject, because we didn't dare tackle the real one. The truth was his parents depressed me and mine made him feel like the invisible man. It wasn't anything any of them did deliberately, which made it worse. I was always looking for some chance to bring

148

Bo Jo and my parents closer together, in the hopes that when my parents knew him better they'd like him better.

Every year on the Fourth of July, which is also my birthday, Mother and Father pack up a picnic lunch and we all, including Grandmother Greher, drive forty miles to Cain Island, a small island reached by a lumpy oyster shell causeway. Some distant relative left it to Father in his will. He's never done anything about selling it or developing it because he says that every man needs an island all his own with nothing on it but trees and brush. This island also had marsh grass and a quarter of a mile of hard white sand on the ocean side. Truthfully, for the past few years I hadn't looked forward to the day. The high school group had its own picnic out at Archer's Pond, and I hated missing that. Also the fun I'd used to have with Grace and Gory, rushing madly around looking for shells, tumbling in the surf, no longer was fun. If my parents made me go I'd take a book and wander off by myself or concentrate on getting an even tan. However, this year I looked forward to showing Bo Jo the island; I even thought a whole day's outing with my family would bring them to appreciate him more. He is a marvelous swimmer and can build a fire by just breathing on a piece of wood.

A note from Grandmother Greher about a week in advance invited Bo Jo and me to ride with her in the Lincoln, which suited me just fine. She was the only person in the crowd that truly liked Bo Jo, though Grace was beginning to warm up a little. I should have waited and asked Bo Jo about it . . . I hadn't even told him about our Fourth of July picnics . . . but I didn't. I rushed right over to Hatty Barnes' and called Grandmother Greher and told her we'd love to. I honestly thought we would. When Bo Jo got home I showed him her note as though I were making him a present.

"What's this Fourth of July bit?" he said.

"It's a family picnic, a kind of tradition. We always go to the island on the Fourth."

"But we can't," Bo Jo said. "I've already told my folks we'll eat with them. My sister Alice from Atlanta will be home. Ma's been cooking all week."

"Oh, no! Why didn't you tell me?"

149

"Why didn't you tell me what *you* were up to?"

"I wasn't *up* to anything. I didn't think anything about it one way or another. It's something we *always* do. I thought you'd enjoy it. You love the beach. . . ."

"Sure, sure. I'd like to go there with you some day but not with your whole family. Anyhow it's no problem. I already told Ma, like I said, that we'd be there. It means a lot to her."

"It means a lot to my mother too." Actually I wasn't too sure how true this was. Mother could take a picnic or leave it, though anything the whole family did together she liked. She was always saying we didn't do enough together, which was actually nobody's fault but Father's though she made it sound like it was ours. Father liked doing things with us separately, different things with different ones but en masse we confused him.

"But my sister," Bo Jo said. "I should think you'd want to meet her. She sure wants to meet you."

I was curious about his sisters but not that curious. "How long is she going to be here?"

"A couple of days. But that's not the point. Ma's been counting on the Fourth. She's been making a big push for it. She told you! Weeks ago."

"She said your sister was coming but . . ."

"She invited you then to come for the big feed and you said you would."

"But she didn't say *when* it was. Not the exact day. She said your sister was coming the first of July. She didn't say anything about the Fourth."

"Oh, to hell with it!" Bo Jo said, and went over and turned on the stereo. Real high. The Beatles. Nerve-wracking. "So why don't you go with your folks on the picnic and I'll go with mine!" he shouted over the Beatles.

"Great! Then *every*body can be hurt!" I shouted back.

"My folks couldn't be hurt any more than they already are. The way your folks treat them . . . or don't treat them. Ignore them."

"That's not so!" Out of the corner of my eye I saw Hatty Barnes come out of her back door onto the terrace and look up at our window. I dashed over and turned the stereo off. "Hatty Barnes will think we're killing each

150

other," I said, and Bo Jo went and looked out of the window.

"Old snoop," he muttered. I smiled in spite of myself. Who wouldn't have wondered what was going on?

"All I know," Bo Jo said in a calmer voice, "is that I can't let my folks down. That's all I know. They don't have many big things going for them in their life so the little things mean a lot. This Fourth of July get-together means a lot."

"I know what we can do," I said. I wondered why I hadn't thought of so obvious a solution before. "We'll ask them to go with us . . . to the island . . . we'll have a *real* family get-together."

"But all the cooking and stuff Ma's doing . . ." He blushed shyly, "She's even gone and bought a new linen tablecloth."

"The tablecloth will keep. So will the food."

Bo Jo thought this over a minute and then shook his head. "Look, couldn't you just this once go along with me, with my folks? Your idea is fine except for one thing. Your folks aren't going to buy it."

"Of course they will," I said. "You'll see."

"O.K., O.K. Try it for size. But promise me one thing. If your mother isn't a hundred percent for it tell me. *Tell* me. Because if she isn't one hundred percent I don't want my folks embarrassed."

I agreed that I didn't want his family made uncomfortable any more than he did. I decided not to take the subject up with Mother over Hatty Barnes' telephone so I went around to the house right after breakfast the next morning. I'd forgotten it was Saturday because it was the end of the month and Bo Jo had had to work at the bank. Grace and Gory were still hanging around the breakfast table eating sweet rolls and drinking coffee. The more the baby showed the more self-conscious I found I was with Grace. Grace had never mentioned anything to do with the subject. I thought at first maybe she just hadn't noticed, but when I went into maternity clothes and she still didn't say anything I knew it was because she didn't want to. She was probably remembering the remarks that had been made at high school and how mad she'd been at the girls who'd made them. She was probably feeling personally humiliated.

They looked up kind of startled when I walked in. Gory said, "Hi. Did you come over to go to the game with us?"

"What game?"

"Mine. Little League," Gory said.

I took a roll, and Mother walked in from the kitchen with a cup of coffee.

"What brings you out so early?"

"Drink your coffee. It can wait," I said. For some reason I didn't want to go into my problem with Gory and Grace sitting there all ears."

"But as soon as I've finished we're going out to watch the Little League game. If Gory's team wins this one it puts them in the running for the final play-off."

"State champion maybe," Gory said. "Why'nt you come?" He was looking at me with the old half-pleading, half-teasing look.

"Yes, why don't you?" Mother echoed. "Do you good to get some sun and fresh air."

"But I haven't even washed the breakfast dishes."

"It won't hurt to forget them this once," Mother urged. "It's quite an occasion. A lot of your friends will be there. Even Grace is going."

"It's the 'in' thing to do on Saturday morning now," Grace said, and added, "But I'm not going. I've changed my mind."

"Aw, you gotta," Gory said. "Besides, I heard you telling someone you'd see them there."

"I am not going," Grace repeated, flushing, and suddenly jumped up and left the room. Mother and Gory looked flabbergasted, but I knew what the matter was. I followed her out onto the sun porch where she was swinging madly in the couch swing.

"Just for your information," I said, "I'm not about to go to the silly old game. So relax and worry not. I won't disgrace you."

I'd really hit the nail on the head because Grace burst into tears. "I can't help it," she cried, "I can't help the way I feel."

"Neither can I," I said, "and right now I hate you." I

152

stomped back into the dining room. Gory and Mother were scurrying around clearing the table.

"What I came to ask you," I said bluntly, "was if Bo Jo's mother and father and sister could come to the Fourth of July picnic." Mother stopped dead in her tracks, her lips slightly parted and I hurried on. "Because if they can't, we've got to go to their house on the Fourth. Bo Jo's sister is going to be here for the weekend and he promised them a long time ago. . . ."

"Why, of course, dear," Mother said. "Why, yes indeed. Do you want me to call them or will you tell them?"

"I think you'd better call them," I said.

"Very well. Yes, yes . . . of course. Why certainly."

I remembered what Bo Jo had said about the hundred percent bit, but how could I tell? Besides, it was too late to back out now.

The day of the Fourth began with a huge thunderstorm. Bo Jo and I lay in bed listening to the rain and counting between the thunder and the lightning flashes to see how close the center of the storm was to us. There was one clap that sounded like one of Hatty Barnes' trees had been hit, which took me into Bo Jo's bed in one jump.

"Maybe the picnic is off," Bo Jo said hopefully.

"Never," I said. "That's part of the tradition."

However, the storm was over and a hot sun steaming down by the time we set out. The Joneses insisted on taking their own car for which I didn't blame them. They didn't want to be divided up between Father and Grandmother Greher. They didn't know the way and the first plan was that we'd all trail along together in a sort of caravan, but Grandmother Greher refused. She never explains anything or makes excuses, so I don't know why she refused, but I think it probably had to do with the way she drives, which is like fast. Bo Jo had never driven with her before, and for the first five miles or so I could see he was pretty electrified but when he realized that Grandmother Greher wasn't just an eccentric old lady playing Russian roulette with the traffic but a quick-witted driver with a firm hand on the wheel and eyes to the right and left, he relaxed. She used to ride horseback a lot when she was younger and I think driving her car as though both it and she have to give a peak preformance sort of makes up for not being able to ride anymore. Of course we reached Cain Island before anyone else and by the time the others got there Bo Jo had already dug a pit for the fire we would build on the beach, and Grandmother Greher with her binoculars swinging from her shoulder was out of sight, looking for curlews.

Bo Jo's sister, Alice had gotten in late the night before and hadn't seen him yet. She hugged him and dabbed at her eyes and couldn't seem to find anything to say for a minute as though he'd been lost or off to war and she was surprised to find him whole and healthy. Bo Jo, looking somewhat embarrassed but also pleased, backed off and said, "This is July. I want you to meet her."

There was pride in his voice, and I remember thinking, "Well, that's something new," and liking the way it made me feel. I shook hands with Alice and she said she was glad to meet me because she'd heard so much about me, to which I never can find an answer and didn't even try to but I liked her handshake, which was cool and firm, and her eyes, which were soft and shy.

While these introductions were going on, Father was unloading our car and Mr. and Mrs. Jones theirs. Out of the corner of my eye I saw Grandmother Greher returning from her bird hunt and remembered suddenly, wretchedly, her once saying that she could tell all there was to know about people by the sort of things they took on a picnic. "Some, you know," she said, "bring such a clutter of things you wonder why they didn't stay home where they can be truly comfortable without all the fuss and the fetching and carrying." At the time she'd been speaking in praise of Mother's single carryall, which never looked as though it could hold enough for our beach-whetted appetites but always did—a jug of lemonade, a bottle of wine for the grown-ups, bunches of grapes, several pounds of ground steak to be cooked on a sheet of tin over the fire and a loaf of homemade bread sliced to sop up the gravy ... that was all, ever. Father walked past us with the carryall. Mrs. Jones followed with a huge casserole which Bo Jo tried to take from her saying, "Let me help," but she clutched it all the more firmly.

"There's plenty more you can bring in the car," she said.

154

"Plenty more," Mr. Jones repeated after her. He was carrying a case of beer and a large covered basket. I wandered down to the beach. Mother had taken off her shift and was lying in her bathing suit face down in the sand. Father was at the ocean edge with Gory and Grace. As Mrs. Jones put down her casserole dish next to the carry-all, Mother opened one eye and said, "Mmmmm. Smells good." She opened the other to see Mr. Jones deposit the beer and the picnic basket and said, "Goodness." By the time Bo Jo and Alice had emptied the car, she was propped on one elbow looking at two folding cots, a beach bag, another hamper of food, two blankets, a pillow, a beach umbrella which Bo Jo was trying to open and a transistor radio which Alice still held in her hand tuned to the twelve o'clock news. Grandmother Greher was fast approaching from the west and Father, confused by the strange voice coming out of Alice's transistor, came striding up from the water's edge to see who it was that had crashed our party. They arrived at the same moment. Fortunately the Joneses were too occupied with setting up cots, umbrellas, and getting out sun lotion to notice the look that passed between my parents or to hear Grandmother's quick intake of breath as she peered down into an open basket containing a collection of movie magazines which I could only hope belonged to Alice if they had to belong to anyone. It was I who blushed. For myself? For Bo Jo? For his family? Or for mine because the Joneses were, after all, their guests, and should not be made fun of however privately or subtly. I tried to catch my mother's eye to register my disapproval but couldn't as she and Father were still looking at each other in that overly solemn way they have when they're trying not to smile over something.

Unconsciously the Joneses had gathered on one side of a dividing line composed of a couple of food hampers and a beach chair, the Grehers on the other. I now walked around the dividing line and sat down beside Bo Jo's mother on one of the folding cots which Bo Jo's father had set up for her under the umbrella. She was struggling with a bottle of sun lotion, trying to get some of the lotion on her back.

"Let me," I said, and took the bottle from her. I stood

155

up and walked around behind her and began to lather her back. I had never had any physical contact with my mother-in-law before and I was surprised at the warmth of her skin.

However, it was not at her skin that I looked as I, in the center of the Jones camp as it were, administered to her. I looked over her head at my mother and there was that in my look that made her in a moment drop her eyes, and in another moment say, "I do hope you brought some of your fried chicken, Mrs. Jones. July has praised it to the skies."

"Yes indeed," said Mrs. Jones, "I never go on a picnic without a fried chicken or two."

Thinking it over as I barreled home in the back seat of Grandmother Greher's Lincoln beside Alice, whom Grandmother Greher had taken a fancy to, I decided that maybe throwing our two families together wasn't the answer after all, that, in fact, the less they saw of each other the better off Bo Jo and I would be. It was a sad realization.

The summer unwound slowly. Hatty Barnes insisted on giving me a baby shower. She invited a group of her friends and Mother's and Mary Ann for ballast. It was gruesome. I was enthroned in a room full of grown-ups where for almost two hours I untied ribbons and unwrapped tissue paper and tried to find some fresh and charming thing to say about every bottle warmer and nightgown that came along. I felt like the ingenue in an unrehearsed and not very funny comedy. I also felt like a cheat. I mean what had I done to deserve a party in my honor, as it were? I just couldn't get into the spirit of the thing. However, Hatty Barnes had a fine time, and I'm sure picked up enough gossip over the punch bowl to keep her in form for weeks to come.

Later, going over all the loot and putting it away, I said to Bo Jo, "It's highway robbery. That's what it is."

"That's Hatty Barnes' problem, not yours," Bo Jo said, which was actually true and made me feel a lot better about it. The longer we lived together the more we seemed able to sort of build each other up instead of tearing each other down the way we used to.

I got up the morning of the day that turned out to be D day feeling marvelous. It was one of those September mornings that is neither fall nor summer, but you know that summer is over and fall almost here. I was behind on my housework since I'd spent almost the entire day the day before at Bo Jo's mother's sewing things for the baby. I didn't have the heart to tell Mrs. Jones that Mother had already ordered a complete layette from New York including a teddy bear that wound up and played "Baby's Boat Is a Silver Moon."

As soon as Bo Jo left I turned the icebox to defrost and got the laundry together and took it over to dump in Hatty Barnes' washing machine. Hatty Barnes was sitting on the terrace having breakfast and invited me to have a cup of coffee with her. Though I was already practically floating in coffee, it was a small price to pay for the use of her washer. She was wearing the rosebud dress she always wore when she was going to an auxiliary meeting at the church, so I knew it wouldn't be too long.

Looking me over she said, "Well, child, it's not much longer now, is it?"

"About two months," I said.

"Are you planning to keep the apartment for a while after the baby comes?"

"Awhile?" I said. "Goodness, I hadn't even considered ... I mean, you don't have a rule about no children, do you?"

"Of course not," Hatty Barnes said. "Though I imagine when it gets to the toddle stage you may find those steps a hazard. No, it wasn't that made me ask, but somewhere I got the idea that your husband was going back to school after you had the baby. I had that distinct impression from somewhere." She frowned, trying to remember. "Oh, I know who told me. It was your mother's friend, Mary Nobles, at bridge club."

"Well, it would be nice," I said. "And of course some day maybe. But we haven't planned that far ahead. I mean, how can we until we get better situated financially?"

"Oh, I quite understand, but somehow I got the definite impression it had all been arranged. Oh, well, I often get

157

things wrong. It just seemed so logical. I suppose I thought your parents would help."

"Bo Jo would never allow that!" I said. "He's much too proud and independent!"

She smiled and picked her hat off the wrought iron chair where it had been waiting and put it on. "Auxiliary this morning," she said, "and I'm already late. Well, selfishly I'm glad you and your young man will be with me for a while."

When I got back to the apartment Mother was there. She had a letter for me from Horace, and she was looking as grim as was possible for her. I knew she must have wondered about these letters, coming to the old address and addressed to July Greher, but she'd never asked and so I'd thought she either hadn't noticed or was showing a heroic respect for my privacy. But now she handed me the letter as though it were a summons to appear in court, and then she sat down on the sofa and crossed her knees and swung her foot back and forth nervously.

"Well," she said, "aren't you going to read it?"

I could feel myself blushing like a fool. "Not right now if you don't mind," I said.

"I can probably tell you what it says," Mother said. "I had a call from Cecilie Clark this morning. A most upsetting call. She had just received a letter from their nephew Horace asking them if he could stay with them a few days on his way to Princeton. He asked them not to make any plans or engagements for him as he hoped to be spending most of his time with you. Cecilie said he sounded as though it had all been arranged between the two of you. She was baffled to say the very least."

"Nothing had been arranged. I had no idea. . . ." I said. "We just, I just . . ." I stammered and opened the letter and read it.

DEAREST JULY [that was a switch—up until now it had always been "dear"]

With much finagling I've managed it so I can go East a week early. I do hope this is all right with you because I plan to spend most of that week with my aunt and uncle in Trilby.

This letter writing is fine BUT. I will tell you more

about THAT when I see you. I will tell you a lot of other things that can't be put into writing. So R.S.V.P.P.D.Q. as time is of the essence!

In haste and great EXCITEMENT,

With love,

HORACE

"I'll have to write him," I said. "Right away." I was still blushing. "It was just someone to talk to ... about books and things. A sort of pen pal deal. . . ."

"May I see the letter?" Mother said.

Reluctantly I handed it to her. What use to tell her that he'd never called me "dearest" before? And that I'd never even signed my letters "Sincerely yours" much less "With love"?

"My dear," my mother said, handing the letter back to me, "the boy is in love with you, or almost. How *could* you?"

"But it hasn't been like that at all until now. Besides, I thought you knew he was writing to me."

"I'd have to be blind not to but naturally I assumed you'd told him you were married, that you were just pals, pen pals as you put it. He seemed such a nice boy, and you appeared to have so much in common the night he came to our house with Cecilie and Tom and I could understand your writing to each other. I had no idea you were deceiving him."

"Then why did you think the letters came to your house, to July Greher?"

"Because of Bo Jo," Mother said.

"And that didn't bother you?"

"Why should it as long as your friendship with the Clark boy was perfectly innocent? As a matter of fact, I was pleased that you had someone of your own ki—, someone—"

"What you're saying," I interrupted, "is that it is quite all right for me to deceive Bo Jo but not Horace Clark. You may not realize it, but that is what you're saying."

"I abhor deceit in any form," Mother said. "I admit this latest communication from Horace puts a different light on everything, but I couldn't help but be glad that

159

you were keeping some outside contacts." When she saw that I was just looking at her blankly she flushed and said, "You may well need them some day."

And when I continued to stare, she said impatiently, "My darling, surely you and Bo Jo aren't going to feel obligated to stay married forever."

"Sometimes," I said, "you actually shock me. You actually shock me very much."

"I'm sorry," Mother said, and suddenly her eyes filled. "I truly am. But this hasn't been easy for us either. Seeing you changed from a happy carefree child into a troubled nervous sort of premature woman." She dabbed at her eyes with a blue monogrammed handkerchief, tried to smile. "Well, you will write to Horace today, won't you? Air mail. Special delivery. I'll try somehow to explain it to Cecilie."

I started the letter as soon as Mother left. I wrote five different letters, each one longer and more complicated than the last and tore them all up. With every letter I realized more what a cruel and selfish thing I'd done. I also realized how fond I'd got of Horace and how dreadfully I was going to miss his letters.

I got up and put a Beethoven sonata on the stereo, cried for half an hour, and then sat down and wrote:

DEAR HORACE,

I have done a cruel and selfish thing. There is no explaining it except that your letters meant so much to me I couldn't bear to end our correspondence as I have to do now that the whole terrible business has caught up with me. You see, I am married. I've been married for quite some time. I didn't mean to deceive you or even lead you on except in an intellectual way.

I can't expect you to forgive me. Or even not to despise me. Anyway, thank you for being my friend.

Most sincerely and regretfully,
JULY JONES

I took the letter to the post office myself so that I could

buy an air mail and a special delivery stamp. On the way home my back began to ache a little. I'd had backaches before, pressure from my extra weight Dr. Harvey said, so it didn't alarm me, but I was glad to hear a horn toot and see a car pull in at the curb beside me. I saw too late who it was offering me a lift. Alicia Helms, no less. I'd already turned a beaming, grateful smile on whoever it might be and I was stuck with the glad act.

She was driving her mother's sports car. Her hair was a new shade of blond, and her eye shadow was a new shade of green, and she looked like she'd just flown in from Las Vegas. I tried very hard to remember that up until the time I'd started going with Bo Jo I'd liked her fine, but it seemed an awfully long time ago, and the sidewise once-over she was giving me made me feel positively matronly.

"How've you been?" she said. "I haven't seen you in ages. Not since I stopped dating Charlie."

"It's amazing how time flies," I said. "I haven't seen you for ages either."

"Being married is probably a full-time job." She made it sound not only full-time but dreary.

"Oh, I wouldn't put it that way," I said. "Not *all* work and *no* play." She'd asked for it.

"I didn't mean *that*. I just meant I never *see* you and Bo Jo anywhere anymore. Are you headed home? I should have asked."

"Yes," I said.

"Still Hatty Barnes' garage?"

I supposed she wanted to be asked in, but I couldn't face it. I mean I was still burning about the night Bo Jo had gone out on the town, and sure she'd been along.

"Are you going to college this fall?" I tried changing the subject.

"If I live that long. State U. I don't suppose Bo Jo will make it this year. Maybe next, hunh? That football team could certainly use him. Did you see them last year? Sour! Absolutely sour."

We had, thank God, reached Hatty Barnes' driveway. I wondered if my backache were really worse or if I imagined it.

"Thanks a million for the ride," I said.

"You wouldn't have something cool to drink in there, would you? I'm parched."

Some nice tired old arsenic was what I wanted to say. What I did say was, "Could be. Come on up."

Because of spending almost the entire morning on the letter to Horace I hadn't got around to doing anything else. I was sure Alicia would get a bang out of the dirty dishes in the kitchen and last night's mess in the living room. She sat down on the sofa, those green smudged eyes swallowing up every detail like a hungry cat. I went and got us out Cokes, and when I came back she had Bo Jo's trombone lying across her knees running her fingers up and down the keys. The way she touched it was like a caress, and when she looked up at me she smiled a crooked, hurting smile.

"Has he learned yet to play anything beside Ta Ra Boom?"

I shook my head.

"No talent." She picked up the trombone and put it down on the floor beside her and took the Coke I handed her. "But cute though. There was a time when I really could have gone for him and vice versa."

"Why didn't you?" I said coldly.

"I think you know more about that than I do," she said. "After you came along I didn't stand a chance."

"But you've been seeing him still," I blurted. "I know of at least one night. . . ."

"Seeing Bo Jo!" She sounded honestly shocked. "What kind of fool do you think I am?"

"I . . . I . . . don't know, I thought . . ." feeling like every kind of a fool.

"Look." She put her Coke down firmly on the table and got up. "I don't know what *you* thought, but I'll tell you what *I* thought. I thought maybe we could be friends again now that all the shouting's over. We used to be. Remember? O.K., so I was nuts about Bo Jo. What's that got to do with giving you a ride home? Coming up for a Coke?" She grabbed up her cigarettes and made for the door. "All I can say," she said, "is that you must be mighty insecure. That is about all I can say."

I called after her that I was sorry. It seemed to me I

162

was forever calling after someone that I was sorry. But she didn't let on she heard.

When Bo Jo came home I told him I was crying because of my back, because of how it was hurting. Which was partly true. I couldn't eat any supper, and by eight o'clock it was so bad that Bo Jo went over to Hatty Barnes' and called Dr. Harvey. It was while he was gone that I had the hemorrhage.

I'd never been so scared in my life. I thought of course I was going to die. Nobody could lose that much blood and not. My teeth started to chatter, and I tried to pray but I couldn't think of what to pray for. My mind was a quivering blank. When Bo Jo came back I thought for a minute he was going to faint. He turned white and his mouth opened as if he were trying to get air. "Oh my God!" he said, and dashed into the bathroom and came out with a towel, a bottle of iodine and a glass of water, and then he just stared at me not knowing what to do with them.

"Is Dr. Harvey coming?"

"Not right away . . . b-b-because I just told him you had a backache. I thought a backache was all it was."

"Then you'd better call him again," I said.

"I'd better call him again," Bo Jo said, but he didn't move. He seemed rooted to the side of my bed.

"I'll be all right while you're gone," I said.

"Are you having the baby?"

"I don't think so," I said. "There isn't any pain. Just my back hurting."

"Don't move," Bo Jo said. "I'll be right back."

When he came back he said, "Dr. Harvey will be here presto. I also called my mother."

"*Your* mother?"

"She said she'd be right over."

"But I don't want your mother. I want mine." I began to cry.

"I'll go call her," Bo Jo said.

"Not until the doctor gets here."

"As soon as he gets here I'll call her. Are you feeling any better?"

"I think it's stopped."

"What's stopped?" His voice squeaked.

"The bleeding. I wonder what it means."

"The stopping?"

"No, the bleeding."

"Dr. Harvey will know. Would you like some water?"

"I can still feel the baby."

"Well natch. . . ."

"Kicking, I mean. Alive and kicking."

"Is that good?"

Dr. Harvey bustled in just then, beaming and smiling.

"I'll go and call your mother," Bo Jo said.

Still beaming and smiling, Dr. Harvey began to poke and punch and listen with his stethoscope. He then gave me a shot. He then asked questions. He then walked over to the window, looked out, got himself a glass of water.

"What's happened?" I said. "What's gone wrong?"

"Maybe nothing much," he said. "We'll have to see. In the meantime the place for you is in the hospital where you can get flowers and books and boxes of candy. Any objections?"

"Where would they get me?" I said. And soon as Bo Jo came back, Dr. Harvey sent him out again to call an ambulance.

I'd no sooner got settled comfortably in my bed at the hospital than I hemorrhaged again. But by that time thanks to all the shots I'd had things were hazy. The faces of my parents and Bo Jo's parents and Bo Jo, as I was wheeled past them on my way to the operating room, wore the instant smiles of people about to have their picture taken. They seemed a thousand miles away.

They used a spinal anaesthetic because Dr. Harvey said it would be better for the baby, so I knew when they took him and I heard his first cry.

"A boy," Dr. Harvey said, "and so far so good."

"His name is Jonathan," I said, and then they put me to sleep.

I woke up several times before I really came to and each time my mother was there and Bo Jo and a strange nurse. And each time one or the other or all of them said, "Everything is fine. Go back to sleep." When I finally came to only the nurse was there, which was too bad, since I had a lot to talk about. I asked her when I could see my baby, and she said as soon as I could get up and

164

down to the nursery in a wheelchair. He was in an incubator. She said maybe tomorrow. I told her that his name was Jonathan. I told her I'd no idea I'd feel this way about a baby. I told her I felt as if I understood everything and loved everybody. I told her I felt omnipotent. Also ecstatic. Also greatly awed. I told her again that I'd had no idea I'd feel this way. She said it was quite natural. She said it had to do with nature and hormones. I thought it had to do more with God, myself, but that I did not tell her since she obviously had never had a baby and wouldn't know what I was talking about.

I went back to sleep and next time I woke up it was because Bo Jo was saying, "Open your eyes, Mother! You've had more sleep than anybody!"

He was standing beside the bed grinning like a fool. In one hand he carried a toy gun and holster set, in the other the teddy bear Mother had ordered that played "Baby's Boat . . ." and tucked under his arm was a huge bouquet of red roses. He dropped the flowers and the holster on the bed and wound the teddy bear up and sat him on the bureau and then he kissed me.

"You are a brave and wonderful girl," he said.

"I am a woman," I said.

"Does that make me a man?"

"Automatically. Have you seen the baby? What does he look like?"

"Like a baby. A very small baby. A miniature baby. But everything is there. Fingers and toes. Everything."

"What color is his hair?"

"Fuzz color. Dark fuzz. Our mothers say he is beautiful."

"I can't wait to see him. To hold him. Why did they have to operate on me? What went wrong?"

"Dr. Harvey said it was a premature separation of the placenta."

"Meaning?"

"Something to do with the afterbirth. I didn't ask for details. He seemed to think I should know."

"Oh well, all's well that ends well."

"You can say that again!" Bo Jo grinned and went to the bureau and looked in the mirror. "You," he said to his

165

face in the mirror, "are a father. A father of a son. Tr
that on for size!" he said.

Later my mother and father and Grace came. Gory ha
never liked hospitals since he had his tonsils out so h
didn't come, but he sent a model airplane for Jonathan
one that he'd been working on for weeks and just finished

"You look much too young to be a grandmother,"
told Mother.

"After last night," she said, "I feel old enough to be
great-grandmother."

"You gave us quite a scare," Father said.

"I also gave you a consolation prize," I said. "How do
you like him?"

"It's not fair," Grace said. "You always did get the
prettiest doll."

"He is adorable," Mother said.

"What there is of him," Father said.

"Come now, Paul," Mother said. "According to Mothe
Greher you didn't weigh much more than that when yo
were born, and look at you now."

While they were still there Bo Jo's mother came. She
brought me a lemon custard, a tiny blue sweater with
matching bootees which she had knitted, and a book
called *Prayers for New Mothers*.

After that the nurse said no more visitors except my
husband, but the room began filling up with flowers like a
garden in full bloom.

"I feel," I told Bo Jo, "like a prima donna on opening
night."

It was a wonderful day, a beautiful day, and Dr. Harvey said that in the morning the nurse could wheel me
down to the nursery. I went to sleep feeling satisfied and
complete.

I saw my baby just that once. Through a pane of
glass. I thought him quite perfect. His skin was clear and
only faintly pink, and his head was round and even. I
thought him quite perfect, but apparently he wasn't. Late
that afternoon Dr. Harvey told me that he had developed
some trouble with his breathing. He said this often happened with premature babies delivered by Caesarian section. He said in this case the chances on his pulling out of
166

it were good because his overall condition was good. I wasn't worried.

The next morning the nurse told me that he was "holding his own." I didn't like the sound of that.

I said, "You mean he's not much better but he's no worse?"

"I mean," she said, "that he's holding his own."

I wanted to go down and see him at once. As the nurse was helping me up, she said, "I think you should know they've put a pin in his chest to help with his breathing. I thought I should explain so you wouldn't be startled by it."

"A pin *into* his chest?"

"No, just through the skin to lift the chest wall. It does look a little alarming, but it is a help to him."

"I don't think I want to see him after all," I said. "I don't think I could bear it."

"Perhaps I shouldn't have told you," the nurse said. "It's not as bad as it sounds."

"If I could pick him up, hold him, comfort him, it would be different," I said, "but to just look and not be able to help . . ."

"I quite understand," the nurse said.

When Bo Jo came in on his way to work, I could tell that he'd stopped by the nursery first. He looked pale and anxious and kept telling me in a hearty voice not to worry.

I worried all day and all night. I worried up until eleven A.M. the next morning when Dr. Harvey and Bo Jo came to tell me that the baby was dead.

Everybody said I took it very well. That was because I didn't cry. I didn't cry because I was still feeling the joy and the wonder of his birth, and his death had no reality for me. So maybe he wasn't down the hall in the nursery, but that didn't make him not anywhere. Or just plain NOT. It was my first close personal contact with death, and the whole thing was incomprehensible. I had never held him or spoken to him so my feeling about him was all I'd ever had, and I still had that. That is why, at the time, I didn't cry.

Bo Jo cried. He knelt down by the side of my hospital bed like a child about to say his prayers and buried his

167

head in his arms and sobbed. He said maybe we should have had the expensive doctor, maybe then this wouldn't have happened. I told Bo Jo I didn't think it would have made any difference who we had.

Mother also cried because "he was so little and helpless," and Father gave me a gold wristwatch, some French perfume, and called me "Ducky," which he hadn't done since I was ten and begged him not to.

Bo Jo's mother cried and talked about "God's will" and "the Kingdom of Heaven," while his father kept his back to us and looked out the hospital window and now and then blew his nose.

Grandmother Greher didn't cry. She didn't even mention the baby. She came and sat beside my bed and read aloud to me from *Mountain Interlude* by Robert Frost until I went to sleep.

The day before I went home Mary Ann came and sat on the end of my bed and did her nails and talked very fast about a marvelous movie she'd seen and a marvelous book she'd read and a marvelous party she'd been to until the nurse told her she thought I was getting tired. Which I was.

"I'm real sorry about the baby," she said, just as she was leaving. "But at least now you'll be able to go back to school and everything."

I just barely managed to hold myself together until she got out of the door, and then I let loose. I cried and sobbed until finally the nurse made me take some pills to stop it. Even then I wasn't crying because our baby died, but because Mary Ann so obviously thought of him as just an accident that never should have happened, and I realized a lot of other people probably thought the same thing and now neither he nor we could ever prove how wrong they were.

I went home to Mother and Father's house the next day. I wanted to go home to our apartment, but Mother, Father, the doctor, and even Bo Jo insisted I'd get back on my feet a lot faster with someone to look after me. I didn't fight it. I was feeling shaky in more ways than one. And I thought it would be only for a week. And I'm sure that at that time Bo Jo thought so too.

Mother had had my room painted while I was in the

hospital and new curtains made and a new ruffly bed-spread. Aside from that nothing was changed. Cards from high school dances and snapshots of Mary Ann and Tommy Ryan and Charlie Saunders were still stuck around the edges of the mirror. My foreign doll collection was still arranged on the top shelf of the bookcase.

Father and Bo Jo made a chair of their hands and lifted me downstairs for supper. There were flowers on the table and at my place a finger bowl filled with blue forget-me-nots, Grace's contribution, and home-churned ice cream for dessert, Gory's offering. Everyone talked at once as though I'd been away on a long journey and hadn't heard any news of them for months. Their pleasure at having me home again was touching, but I couldn't get into the spirit of the thing. My room all redone and waiting for me, this festive supper, gave me the uneasy feeling that, in some way which they were hardly aware of, this was a celebration. I kept looking across the table at Bo Jo, but he was thoroughly enjoying the roast duck and spinach soufflé and appeared for the first time quite at ease with my family. A few weeks ago this would have made me very happy.

The really panic moment came when it was time for me to go upstairs to bed and for Bo Jo to go home to the apartment. I don't know why it should have seemed any different from all those nights in the hospital when it came time for him to leave, but it did. Entirely different. I mean, it suddenly dawned on me why couldn't he have stayed here while I had to stay here? I mean wouldn't that be only natural? It wasn't as though there weren't room enough. But this apparently hadn't occurred to either my parents or Bo Jo, and so I didn't bring it up. But it hung there, a great big fat question in my mind long after I went to bed.

It seems funny that I didn't get the drift right away. I mean as soon as the baby died. Or when Mary Ann spelled it out for me that day at the hospital. "At least now you'll be able to go back to school and everything."

The second night after I got home Bo Jo came again for supper which I naturally assumed he would, but apparently nobody else had. At the last minute I saw Mother surreptitiously setting an extra place for him. I was glad

169

Bo Jo didn't see it, because it would have hurt his feelings.

That night when it was time to go to bed I asked Bo Jo to come upstairs and tell me good night. Father put down his paper and looked at Mother and cleared his throat, and Mother said to me, "It's late and you look awfully tired, dear," and to Bo Jo, "Don't you think she looks tired?"

Bo Jo grunted something that could have been "yes" or "no" and I said, "He won't stay long."

Father said, "Dr. Harvey distinctly told us . . ."

"Look," I said, "Bo Jo and I haven't exchanged two words in private for two whole days," I said. "After all, he *is* my husband."

"Of course, dear," Mother said, and flushed.

"Look," Bo Jo said, when we got out in the hall, "couldn't we maybe talk on the sun porch. They've made such a production of the whole thing I feel like a fool."

We went and sat on the porch in the swing in the dark, and Bo Jo put an arm around me. "Do you miss me?" I said. "At the apartment?"

"Yeah," he said. "It's not the same place. As a matter of fact it got so bad I didn't see any point in going back there last night. I spent the night with my folks."

"How are they?"

"Fine."

I could feel his arm around my shoulder tense, and I said, "What did you talk about?"

"Nothing much. We watched television mostly."

"I bet they talked to you about going back to school, didn't they?"

"How did you know?" His arm now felt stiff and uncomfortable to me.

"It figures," I said. "It's in the air. I feel it all around me. Your parents. My parents."

"I told them I didn't want to talk about it. Not right now."

"Not right now?"

"I don't think we're in any shape right now," he said.

"For school? Or to talk about it?"

"For any damned thing!" He drew his arm back, away

170

from me. "You're almost as bad as they are. What's eating you?"

"I'm scared," I said.

"Of what?" Bo Jo said.

"I don't know yet. I just got that way."

"If it's them you're scared of, don't be. They can't do anything we don't go along with." He put his arm back around me, tighter than before, and with his other hand pulled my head down onto his shoulder.

I didn't say anything and in a little while he said, "You know, when you asked me what our baby looked like and I said 'like a baby,' I was just trying to play it cool. Trying not to be corny. Frankly, I thought he was pretty cute. His ears especially."

"His ears?"

"Yeah, the way they were fastened onto his head. Close. Not like mine."

"What I liked," I said, "were his hands. Did you notice his hands?"

"Miniature hands. What I don't understand is how I can miss something I never had. How I can go around feeling like my guts are hanging out on account of a baby I hardly had time to say 'hello' to. And it's worse for you. Ten times worse. Carrying him around inside you all that time."

"At least I got to know him a little. No one around here has even mentioned him since I got home. It's eerie."

"They probably think it would upset you to talk about him."

"Not talking about him upsets me more. As though he'd never been."

"Well, he was!" Bo Jo said.

And there was Mother standing in the doorway looking anxious and saying, "It's almost eleven o'clock."

Two days before I was to go back to the apartment Mother announced, oh so casually, that she had asked Bo Jo's parents to drop in after supper for coffee. I knew very well that Mother would as soon entertain one hundred people for dinner as spend an evening with the Joneses.

I said, "What's the pitch going to be? I do think Bo Jo and I should be given a little warning."

"Pitch?" Mother said.

"Yes, the angle. As to our future. That is why you're having them, isn't it? To talk about US."

"Not to talk *about* you," Mother said, "to talk *with* you."

"About what?"

"You sound so defensive, dear," Mother was washing the breakfast dishes and I was drying them. She scooped a handful of flat silver out of the suds and dropped them noisily into the rinsing pan. "We only want to help."

"With what?"

"Well, the situation *is* different now. Surely you and Bo Jo will want to reevaluate . . ."

"Of course. Eventually. But why right now? This minute? Before we've had a chance to get over the baby, sort things out, talk things over between us . . . I mean, why the big rush?"

"There's no big rush," Mother said, "except that . . . oh, dear, why must we go into this now?"

"Except that what?" I persisted.

"Except that we do not think you should return to your apartment until you've come to some decision about the future. Do you?"

"Why not? What on earth has that got to do with it?"

"Everything," Mother said. "How could you and Bo Jo be expected to make a truly detached and intelligent decision while you're still living together as man and wife? And then too," she said, and actually blushed, "there's always the possibility of another baby."

She had me there because the truth was now that she'd said it I realized that in my heart of hearts that is exactly what I wanted. I wanted to go back to the apartment and start another baby. Only I didn't think of it like that. I thought of it as getting our lost baby back. That's how I thought of it and that was what I wanted to do. Crazy. Selfish even. But I couldn't help it. I suppose it was nature talking. Nature, they say, abhors a vacuum. And I was a vacuum.

"You are cruel!" I cried to my mother. "You don't understand!" I sobbed and threw down the soggy dish towel and dashed out of the kitchen and upstairs to my room and locked the door.

She came a little later and knocked. I told her that I

172

was sorry I'd howled at her, but I didn't open the door. I told her I was resting.

I thought off and on all day about calling Bo Jo at the bank, but what could I say? He probably already knew about the grand conclave tonight. And even if he didn't, what good would it do to tell him? As he'd said, they couldn't do anything we didn't go along with. But what was to stop us from going along with them? What in the name of common sense, logic and just plain fair play was there to stop us? If there was nothing to stand between me and their rosy plans for our salvation, there was even less from Bo Jo's point of view. Even less than nothing.

In the end Bo Jo called me. He called from a pay station at the bank, and there was such a humming in the phone that we both had to say everything over two or three times.

He said, "What's this big get-together all about?"

"Us, of course."

"What about us?"

"We've been given a reprieve, didn't you know?"

"A what?"

"A reprieve. A second chance. Freedom!"

"Is that what you want?"

"I want what you want."

"So that makes us tie."

"I mean it. I want whatever you want. But I've got to know what it is," I said, "I've got to know before tonight."

"I think you need me," he said. "Right now especially. Maybe later on . . ."

I felt tears rush to my throat and blood to my head. I said, "Don't be silly. Need, need, need, what kind of a stupid basis is that? So we get married out of necessity, and we stay married out of need. Great! What about love, Bo Jo? How do we stand on love?"

"You sound bitter," Bo Jo said. "You sound mad."

I took a deep breath and counted to ten and let my breath out slowly. "Maybe I am," I said, "but not with you, not about you. Nobody can say you didn't try, nobody can say we didn't."

"Don't sound so damned final," Bo Jo said. "Nothing's settled yet. Not by a long shot."

"I think you'll find," I said, "that it is." I then hung up and went back to my room and looked over my clothes closet trying to decide what to wear to the inquisition.

The Joneses arrived at eight on the dot. I could tell from the easy way they greeted Mother and Father that there must have been preliminary meetings and talks, because there was no longer any awkwardness between them. It was the first slightly chill evening, and Mother served the coffee in front of the fire in Father's study. It got to be quarter past eight and still no Bo Jo. The small talk was beginning to wear thin, and my head was beginning to ache. At twenty minutes past Bo Jo got there. His face had the slightly disheveled look of someone who has been sleeping or crying or maybe drinking. He drank the coffee Mother gave him in one gulp, standing up. There was only one empty chair left in the room, a straight-back beside the love seat where his parents were sitting. When he'd finished his coffee, he went and sat crouched on the edge of it and looked at me and tried to smile, but it didn't quite come off.

I had expected Father would deliver the first speech, but it was Mr. Jones who said, "No point in beating around the bush. You kids probably know we're here to help you get straightened out, back on the right track. Right?"

Bo Jo nodded. I didn't even do that.

"Not that we aren't sorry about how things turned out, but nobody could help that. No sense in crying over spilled milk. The thing is to look ahead. Think about the future. Right?"

"You are so young," Mother said, "still children really, with so much to look forward to."

"For children," Bo Jo said, "we've been through a lot."

"But there's a lot you haven't been through," Father said. "School, for one thing. And a chance to be young, for another."

"Everyone," Mother said, "should have a chance to be young."

"Especially," Mrs. Jones said, "a pretty girl like July."

"And everyone should have a chance to finish school," Mother said, "especially a capable, ambitious boy which Bo Jo has certainly proved himself to be."

174

The duet bit was too much.

"Let's get it over with," I said. "What are your rosy plans for our future?"

"Perhaps you don't realize it," Father said, "but you are being impertinent. We aren't here to force you into anything. We are only here to help you decide what is best."

"Like what are the choices?" Bo Jo said.

"Why kid 'em?" Mr. Jones said. "Why kid 'em along? There aren't any choices. Either you stay in the rut you're in the rest of your life or until this little girl here gets tired of playing house with a guy who never finished high school and calls it quits, or you go back to school like you planned before any of this came up."

"What about July?" Bo Jo said. "Where does she fit in?"

"She fits in," Father said, "where she belongs, in a good girls' school and then in a good girls' college."

"Married girls can't go to high school," I said.

"We weren't thinking of *this* high school, dear," Mother said. "We were thinking of Miss Fairworth's School near Providence."

"They don't allow married girls in boarding schools either," I said.

"We weren't thinking in terms of your being married," Father said very quietly, and I could feel everybody brace themselves for the crisis.

"That's what I figured," I said, and looked at Bo Jo. He was looking at me, but like always I couldn't tell what he was thinking. "What are you thinking, Bo Jo?" I said.

"I'm thinking we need time," Bo Jo said. "I'm thinking this is a railroad job."

"Also it is something we should discuss by ourselves. Just between us," I said.

"Of course," Mother said, "but as I told July today I don't think you should go back to the apartment until you've come to a decision."

"Why not?" Bo Jo said, and when no one said anything he began to get red around the ears. "Why not?" he said again.

"The birds and the bees," I said. "They're scared of them."

"It's only common sense," Mrs. Jones said. "It's all we

175

ask of you and little enough under the circumstances. . . ."

"But you can have all the time to decide that you want," Father said, "all the time in the world."

"I don't know about that," Mr. Jones said. "If Bo Jo's going to make the University by the second quarter he's got to get moving soon. He's still got high school credits to get."

"I think," I said, "if you'll excuse me I'm going to bed."

Bo Jo followed me out into the hall and hung over the banister as I went up the stairs.

"Look, honey. Let's think about this good now. Let's not let them railroad us into something. . . ."

"They aren't railroading us," I said. "They're right, that's all. They're so damned right I could scream. And you know it, Bo Jo. You know it even better than I!"

"I don't know anything," Bo Jo said. "My head's in a swivet."

"And how's your heart?" I said.

"It's in a swivet, too," he said.

"Thanks," I said. "I think I can sleep on that."

And I did sleep on it for a while. I dreaned I was playing in the carriage house at Grandmother Greher's, hide-and-seek with Grace and Gory. I must have been about eight or ten because my hair was in pigtails and my dress was above my knees. I was hiding up on a rafter watching them scurrying around below looking for me. They finally gave up and decided to go and pick blueberries. I scrambled down and went running out into the sunshine after them crying their names and asking them to wait for me. I woke up out of breath and turned on the light. I'd forgotten that a light turned on anywhere in the house in the middle of the night brought Mother running. Even in her sleep she keeps a kind of radar going. She was wearing a lavender robe, and her hair and eyes were fuzzy with sleep.

"Are you all right?" It was what she always said, and for a minute I didn't remember that I was no longer a child.

"No," I said. "I'm scared."

"Of what?" Mother said, and tried to take my hand,

but then I remembered. Everything. I pulled my hand away.

"Nothing," I said. "It was just a dream."

"Would you like a snack? Some milk? Crackers?"

"No, thank you."

"Darling," she said, "you know we would give you the moon if we thought it was good for you, right for you."

"I know," I said. And I did. That was the worst of it.

"We love you so very much." She leaned down and kissed my cheek. "And want to take care of you. That's all it amounts to." I felt a tear drop out of her eyes onto my forehead. "If you truly love Bo Jo and he you ... maybe in time . . ."

"What is truly love, Mother?" I said. "Just what is it?"

"At sixteen, darling, I don't know. I just don't know."

"Neither do I," I said, "not that it matters. . . ."

Bo Jo called on his lunch hour the next day just as usual. And came by after work just as usual. Though it wasn't mentioned, the Big Decision hung over us like a cloud, and we were tense and cross with each other.

Nor did we mention the fact that tomorrow was supposed to have been my big homecoming day. I hardly slept at all that night, and the next noon when Bo Jo called I asked him to meet me at the Coffee Pot when he got off work. I was strong enough now to go out, and I was beginning to go stir crazy. He said he'd pick me up at the house, but that would have meant walking, and I didn't feel quite that strong yet.

Bo Jo was already there when I got there. He'd nailed us a booth at the very back and had already had one cup of coffee and smoked, I could see from the ashtray, three cigarettes.

I said, "You're going to have to cut down on these when you go back to school." Meaning the cigarettes.

He said, "I'm going to have to cut them out, period." And then we looked at each other, realizing what we'd said, realizing that it had all been settled and we knew it and had probably known it all along. He put his hand over mine on the table top and for a minute we just went on looking at each other, smiling in a weak kind of way.

177

"A girl like you," he said, "should have lots of fun and boys to take her pick from before she settles down. . . . I found those letters in your bureau drawer . . . to somebody named Horace. I read them. Also yours to him."

"Oh," I said, and "Oh" again. Bo Jo stared at the end of his fourth cigarette and said nothing.

"When did you find them?"

"The night after the baby died. That night."

"Oh God! I'm so sorry! They didn't mean anything. I swear it."

"I wanted to be by myself that night," Bo Jo said, as though he hadn't heard me. "I went over to the apartment and sat around awhile playing the stereo, just sort of sat around. After a while I got this idea, this crazy idea that I wanted him . . . the baby . . . to wear something of his own when they buried him . . . not just any old whatever they had on him in the hospital . . . so I went rooting through your drawers looking for one of those dresses you had put away for him . . . and, I found the letters!"

"Please, Bo Jo . . ." I put my hand over his where it lay on the top of the table. "I hardly knew Horace. The letters were a sort of game or something. . . . They meant absolutely nothing!"

"They meant that you were lonely," Bo Jo said, and brought his eyes up to meet mine, those living-color eyes that I still could not read.

"I hardly remember. It was so long ago."

"Not *so* long ago."

"When it *started* was long ago. . . . It was just one of those things that got going and I didn't know how to stop. . . . When it started was before I even *felt* married. Maybe I *was* lonely then . . . but there's no excuse, I know. . . . I . . . I . . ."

"Look, July, I'm not holding court. Honest. Maybe we both need to live it up a little. . . ."

"Those damned letters!" Tears were beginning to run out of my eyes and down my face. And they weren't just tears for me but for him too. I could see him sitting in our bedroom, hunched under the light on the night table, alone, defenseless. . . . "I never meant to hurt you . . ." I blubbered. He pulled out a handkerchief and handed it to
178

me. It was clean and white and neatly pressed . . . not like the ones I laundered for him. The tears fell faster.

"Oh hell, the letters don't matter. What matters is now. What we do now," he said.

"Yes, I know." I pulled myself together. I even smiled. "I'm really honestly glad you've got a chance to go to college. A boy like you should most absolutely go to college. I always did feel terrible about that."

"Oh, we would have got around to that eventually, I think," Bo Jo said. "I mean honestly I think if things hadn't happened like they did, we would have made it you and me. . . ."

"Because we would have had to," I said.

"And now we don't. . . ."

"And so it isn't fair. . . ."

"Not to anybody. . . ."

I drank my coffee. I drank it slowly because after I finished it then what?

Bo Jo said, "I hope we can see each other once in a while. I mean I think we really should."

"I don't think it would be very smart," I said, "I mean, I don't think it would work. It . . . it didn't before, remember, and we'd given our solemn word. . . ."

"Maybe we can talk on the phone," he said. "I'm going to miss you. It doesn't seem natural to just cut everything off bang."

"It isn't natural," I said. "None of it. The getting married. The getting unmarried. So there's no sense in trying to treat it that way. No sense at all." I was afraid if I stayed much longer I'd start bawling out loud, and I didn't want to do that. Not at this point. I looked at my watch. "I've got to run," I said. "I promised Mother I'd have her car back."

I jumped up, and Bo Jo jumped up. He followed me out to the car and opened the door, and when I was inside closed it and leaned in the window and kissed me, and I started the motor and drove home. Neither one of us said "Good-bye." It was all very undramatic and insignificant, and I didn't feel like crying anymore.

Mother was all dressed up and waiting for her car when I got home, but she took one look at me and decided not

179

to go wherever it was she'd been planning to go. She said, "Darling, what is it? You look ill."

"It's nothing I won't get over," I said, and tried to walk past her and upstairs to my room, but she came and put her arms around me and drew my face down against her shoulder and smoothed my hair the way she used to do when I was little and had hurt myself.

"You've seen Bo Jo?"

"Yes," I said, "and it's all over." Saying it made it almost real and with my mother's arms around me it didn't seem like so big a tragedy after all.

"You won't be sorry," my mother said, and I could almost believe her.

I kept very busy the next few weeks. Mother saw to that. And the news traveled fast. I guess Mother saw to that too. Mary Ann called and asked me to go to the movies with her and Alan, who was in town. Bo Jo wasn't mentioned all evening.

Mother and Father poured over brochures from Northern boarding schools and asked for my opinion on various ones. I said whatever they decided would be all right with me.

Mother and I went to Savannah one day to shop for school clothes. "The sky's the limit!" Mother said gaily. I made a real effort to join into the spirit of the thing and came home with a wardrobe that would have cost Bo Jo a month's salary at the bank. I put on one of the dresses, a lovely rose-colored silk shift, and my pearls and came down to dinner in it. It was pathetic how happy it made everybody to see me "taking an interest in life" again. I hadn't realized what a drag I'd been on the whole household. We had sherry on the closed porch before we ate and even Gory was allowed a glass.

"Just like old times." Father beamed.

"You never looked lovelier," Mother said.

"You are a wonderful family," I said.

It was all true.

I received a note from Grandmother Greher inviting me to go to the mountains with her for a week in October. I hadn't seen her since the day she came to the hospital and

180

read Robert Frost to me so I decided to drive out to Holly Hill and tell her I'd love to go to the mountains except that I was going away to boarding school.

When I got there, she was in the kitchen preparing to make apple cider. Her sleeves were rolled up above the elbows and the skin hung away from her arms as though it had somehow got loose from the bone . . . an old lady's skin, an old lady's arms. It was the first time I'd ever thought of her as old. It gave me a shaky feeling in the pit of my stomach.

"How are you, child?" The eyes, the smile, weren't old.

"I am missing Bo Jo," I said.

"Here," she said, and shoved a bowl of cooked and wrinkled apples at me, "and here." She gave me a colander and said, "Now the thing is to get out every ounce of juice without completely destroying the pulp. Missing him? You wouldn't be human if you didn't. You'll get over it."

"That's what I'm afraid of," I said, and went to work on the apples. I felt, rather than saw, her pause in her mashing and look at me curiously. I'm sure she wanted an explanation, but I didn't have one.

"Are you coming to the mountains with me? The place where I go has some remarkable fern specimens . . . nowhere else can you find such a variety. I also thought we might take up weaving . . . there's a woman there, a native, who is willing to teach you if she likes you."

"That's what I came to tell you," I said. "I can't." But the rest of the words stuck in my throat. I couldn't say them. Suddenly I put down my bowl. "They want me to go to boarding school," I said, "but I simply can't do it. I'm too old for that. A million light-years too old. I'll take a correspondence course. Go to business school. Night school. Anything but that. It's a phony, that's what it is. I mean, you can't go back to being a teen-ager when you've been a woman for a while. It can't be done. I knew there was something wrong with the whole picture and that's what it is. It's phony!"

"Phony?" Grandmother Greher lifted her eyebrows, clearly snubbing the word but not entirely understanding it.

"False. Illogical. Nuts." I picked up my spatula again and began mashing away at the apples like mad. "Yes, I would love to go to the mountains with you," I said, "and I shall."

"Oh dear," Grandmother Greher sighed, "I didn't mean to interfere. I didn't know you were going away to school."

"You didn't interfere. I simply made a decision, that's all. It's the first decision *I've* made about *anything* in ages."

"I only hope it's a good one," Grandmother Greher said.

"It's a good one for me," I said.

"Those are the only kinds of decisions to make," Grandmother Greher said.

"Not always." I was thinking of Bo Jo and me in the Coffee Pot writing off our marriage.

Telling Mother and Father wasn't as easy as telling Grandmother Greher.

"You're so out of touch," Mother said, "that you don't realize that once you find yourself among girls your own age, doing the sort of things that girls your age should be doing—going to proms, and of course studying—you'll feel entirely differently about it."

"The least you can do," Father said, "is to give it a try. That's not asking too much."

"And that nice Horace Clark will be at Princeton," Mother said, "hardly twenty miles away. . . ."

I didn't tell them that I had heard from "that nice Horace Clark" only the day before, that perhaps unconsciously it had been his letter that had made me see the "phoniness." He had written:

DEAR JULY,

I won't pretend that I understand why you led me on for so long. But I like to think of myself as a fair judge of character and therefore assume you had your reasons, one of which I hope was that you liked me.

My aunt writes that recently you lost a baby. May I offer my most sincere condolences. If you ever find yourself free and unattached again, perhaps we can take up our correspondence where we left off.

Take care,

HORACE

"I was not very nice to that 'nice Horace Clark,' " I said to Mother. "I used him once. I have no intention of using him again."

"*This* would be very different," Mother said.

"No, it wouldn't," I said.

Over my head they exchanged puzzled and exasperated looks. "Then just what do you propose to do?" Father said.

"I want to get the rest of my high school credits . . . maybe through a correspondence school . . . and then I want to take a secretarial course and get a job. I guess what I really want more than anything else is to work things out for myself."

"Your mother has been talking to her!" Mother said to Father. "This sounds exactly like something she would say."

"No," I said, "Grandmother Greher hasn't been talking to me. I've been talking to her."

"It's that boy!" Father exploded. "Have you been seeing him? Have you been in touch with that Jones boy?"

Just like that. In the space of a few weeks Bo Jo, my husband, the father of my lost baby, had become just "that Jones boy."

I opened my mouth to tell them how this shocked and hurt me. But what was the use? That was hardly the point. The point was that we didn't speak the same language anymore, my parents and I. Maybe children aren't supposed to speak the same language as their parents after a certain time. Maybe that's what makes it possible to grow up and leave them.

"No, I haven't seen nor heard from Bo Jo," I said. "Not once," I said, and burst into tears and flew upstairs to my room and barricaded the door.

It was the next day that Hatty Barnes called and said she'd had several inquiries about the garage apartment

183

and when did I plan to give it up. I said I'd get my things out in the next few days. She asked me if that meant Bo Jo's things too, and I said I didn't know, she'd have to ask him. She then said, "Better luck next time," as though I'd lost out at tennis or missed a golf putt.

I kept putting off the apartment bit. Mother wanted to come with me. She was sure I'd overdo, that it was too much for me, et cetera, but I wanted to go alone. I in fact would only go if I could go alone. I felt there would be something almost indecent about taking anyone with me. I couldn't tell Mother this. I didn't really understand it myself. Finally, looking anxious and injured, she let me take her car and go by myself.

I expected the place to be a mess because of all those nights Bo Jo was there alone while I was in the hospital, but it wasn't. There were a couple of dirty cups in the sink and a half-empty Coke bottle on the kitchen table, but aside from that it looked so tidy I thought Bo Jo must already have moved his things out.

However, there was his trombone leaning up against the coffee table in the living room, and there were some shorts and shirts in the soiled clothes hamper in the bathroom and some clean clothes in his bureau drawer. He was, in fact, everywhere I turned. Squatting on the floor hitting sour notes on the trombone, lolloping on the sofa looking at television, dashing from the shower to the bedroom splattering water like a summer rain. Bo Jo with the stubbly hair and the living-color eyes and the stocky, stubborn shoulders. Bo Jo, my husband. Correction. My first husband.

There were some Cokes in the icebox. I opened one and put a Beethoven sonata on the stereo and turned it up as high as it would go and went to work. I started with the bookcase and then the desk and then the bureau drawers. I did all right until I hit the clothes closet ... all those sacky maternity dresses and Bo Jo's old leather jacket with TRILBY HIGH painted across the back. ... I slammed the closet door shut and whirled around, and there was Bo Jo standing in the bedroom door. For real. Him. He was carrying the same old beat-up suitcase of his father's that he'd used to move his things into the apartment and a big cardboard carton.

184

I said, "Fancy meeting you here." But he couldn't hear me because of the Beethoven sonata, and he said something which I couldn't hear either. So I went into the living room and turned the stereo down.

"I saw your car outside," Bo Jo said, "but I came in anyway."

"Why the anyway?" I said.

"You said we shouldn't see each other," Bo Jo said.

"Well, accidents will happen," I said, and wondered why I should sound so cross when actually I was so glad to see him I felt like hugging him.

"Yeah, I suppose we're bound to bump into each other once in a while." He opened up his suitcase and spread it out on the couch and went into the bedroom and came out with an armload of clothes. "Are there any more Cokes in the icebox?" he said.

I got him one and he moved his suitcase over and sat down on the couch.

I said, "I suppose after a while it'll be just like bumping into anyone else," I said. " 'Hi, there,' and 'How's the world treating you?' and all the things people say to each other when they haven't anything to say really."

"I don't believe it," Bo Jo said.

"I don't either," I said.

"I mean," Bo Jo said, "how can two people who've been married to each other, given each other a baby, get to be strangers, total strangers like it just never happened between them?"

"People do it every day," I said, "but I don't understand it."

"I mean," Bo Jo said, just as though I hadn't spoken, "how do you go about scrapping as big a chunk of your life as that? How do you go about it?" He put his Coke down and propped his chin in his hands and looked at me. "How?" he said, and his voice shook, and he was beginning to get red around the ears.

"I've been wondering about that very thing myself," I said. "I suppose like they said the big thing is to concentrate on the future and making good grades and meeting new people, and then, maybe, just maybe, someday, I

185

mean if you, if we, go on feeling like this, about scrapping everything, well, maybe then we can get together again . . . some day . . . when we're sure."

"You know that'll never be," Bo Jo said. "Who's ever sure? Right now we've got something. A relationship. A very close relationship. Maybe we didn't want it but we got it, and we made something of it and it's between us. You and me and nobody else. What's gonna be between us five years from now?"

"I don't know," I said, and began to cry.

"I'm glad you feel that way," Bo Jo said, and gave me his handkerchief, "because that's just how I feel. Exactly."

"But I don't know how I feel."

"You feel like crying," Bo Jo said.

"But I know what we're doing is right, the *right* thing to do. I know that much."

"Whose right thing?" Bo Jo said.

"Everybody's," I said. "Yours. Mine. Theirs."

"Let's leave 'them' out of it," Bo Jo said.

"But we can't. We mustn't. We've hurt them so much already we can't go on hurting them . . . and they'd never understand this . . . not in a million years. . . ."

"What wouldn't they understand?" Bo Jo said, and put his hands on my shoulders and made me look at him, what I could see of him through my veil of tears. "That maybe we've been through things together that we don't *want* to forget. . . ."

"Oh, I don't want to forget any of it . . . not even the fights . . ."

"But we will forget," Bo Jo said, "if we let each other go we will have to. That's why I think it's wrong . . . what they've planned for us. I think it's wrong to let what we have between us go. I know it wasn't much to start with . . . just two crazy mixed-up kids . . . not ready for love much less getting married . . . but we're a lot older than we were a year ago and we mean a lot more to each other than we did then. Doesn't that seem like a hell of a time to get a divorce? Just when we begin to mean more to each other?" He wasn't smiling.

"But we've got to finish school. We owe them that

much." I was trying to be sensible, cautious, but inside I was beginning to sing like a bird.

"We owe ourselves that much too. There are ways ... plenty of them. Not easy but if you want a thing bad enough ..."

"Such as?"

"Such as me swallowing my pride and letting you live with your folks and I live with mine until I finish high school and you take a business course and go to night school so when I go to college you can come along and help support me."

"You seem to have thought the whole thing out," I said.

"That's all I've done since we said good-bye at the Coffee Pot a week ago. Think things out."

"And you weren't even going to *tell* me?"

"Of course I was going to tell you. The first chance I got. I've been hanging around this joint for days waiting for you to come."

"And what if Mother had come with me like she almost did?"

"I would have thought of something," Bo Jo said. "But I had a hunch you'd be by yourself. I had a hunch that would be the way you'd want it."

"You know me so well," I said. And even though there were a few tears still straggling down my face I was smiling at him.

"It's not going to be easy, you know," Bo Jo said, and pulled me down beside him on the couch and held my hand. "Especially for you it's not. It is in fact going to be damned rough in spots."

"I know that," I said, "but this we are doing because we *want* to do it."

"Yeah," Bo Jo said, "and that always helps."

"We *care* now. We care a lot more. At least I do."

"Likewise," Bo Jo said, "but even so we might not make it all the way."

"I know that too," I said, "but then again we just might. And wouldn't that be something!"

"For the books!" Bo Jo said, and we both began to laugh and next thing we were hugging each other and

187

crying like fools. Like a couple of shipwrecked sailors who've just sighted land. Like two people a little bit madly in love.

That was three years ago.... And as Bo Jo said it hasn't been easy, and sometimes it's been downright rough, but here we are! Bo Jo is a junior here at the University, and I've got a job in the bursur's office. Whenever the science lab needs a guinea pig Bo Jo volunteers at a dollar and a half an hour, and when football season is over he chops wood, mows lawns, and clips hedges for some of the faculty. I got my high school diploma and for Christmas Father and Mother treated me to a course in Elizabethan drama, mainly for kicks, but it'll give me a couple of credits if I ever need them.

We live just off campus in the married students' quarters, actually a small pastel box with a picture window looking out on dozens of other pastel boxes in which live dozens of other young couples like ourselves. We call it Culture Alley.

Last weekend I went home to be in Mary Ann's wedding. Bo Jo couldn't get away, and frankly I somewhat dreaded it ... all that white tulle and the Vassar bridesmaids and the ushers driving sports cars and the Bermuda honeymoon and Mary Ann floating on the air of years of anticipation. The what might have been, the can't haves, all spread out before me. But actually once I got caught up in the festivities, the luncheons, the tea dances, the dinners, it was more like a sea voyage than a wistful look-see into never-never-land. There was only one really bad moment, and that was in the church when the music sounded and Alan turned to watch his bride come toward him up the aisle. I didn't look at Mary Ann. I didn't need to. It was all written in Alan's eyes. The joy, the pride. The "I, Allan." The "until death do us part."

I took the bus back to school. I didn't expect Bo Jo to meet me. It was his lab afternoon, and he had a term paper due the next day, but he was there. I saw him before he saw me. His face searching the bus windows looked expectant, impatient, and a little anxious. It was a husband's face. Familiar, known, increasingly beloved.

Mary Ann, I reflected, had an awful lot to learn. And actually, I reflected, I wouldn't be in her shoes right now for all the flowers in Bermuda ... having it all to learn again.